RENEGADE DAWN

BOOK 7 OF THE RENEGADE STAR SERIES

J.N. CHANEY

www.jnchaney.com

1st Edition

For Kamille,

A new friend with an old soul

SERIES BY J.N. CHANEY

The Variant Saga

Renegade Star Series

Renegade Standalones

Orion Colony Series *(with Jonathan Yanez)*

The Last Reaper Series *(with Scott Moon)*

The Fifth Column Series *(with Molly Lerma)*

Resonant Son Series *(with Christopher Hopper)*

Galactic Law Series *(with James S. Aaron)*

Deadland Drifter Series *(with Ell Leigh Clarke)*

Ruins of the Galaxy Series *(with Christopher Hopper)*

Ruins of the Earth Series *(with Christopher Hopper)*

The Messenger Series *(with Terry Maggert)*

Starcaster Series *(with Terry Maggert)*

Sol Arbiter Series *(with Jia Shen)*

Exodus Ark Series

Cyborg Corp Series *(with Chris Winder)*

Wayward Galaxy Series *(with Jason Anspach)*

King's League Series *(with Jason Anspach)*

Orphan Wars Series *(with Scott Moon)*

Sentenced to War Series *(with Jonathan P. Brazee)*

Standalones:

Their Solitary Way

The Other Side of Nowhere

Forever Family

CONNECT WITH J.N. CHANEY

Don't miss out on these exclusive perks:

- Instant access to free short stories from series like *The Messenger*, *Starcaster*, and more.
- Receive email updates for new releases and other news.
- Get notified when we run special deals on books and audiobooks.

So, what are you waiting for? Enter your email address at the link below to stay in the loop.

https://www.jnchaney.com/renegade-subscribe

JOIN THE CONVERSATION

Join the conversation and get updates on new and upcoming releases in the awesomely active **Facebook group**, "JN Chaney's Renegade Readers."

This is a hotspot where readers come together and share their lives and interests, discuss the series, and speak directly to J.N. Chaney and his co-authors.

facebook.com/groups/jnchaneyreaders

CONTENTS

IMPORTANT CHARACTERS AND TERMS

Humans

Jace Hughes : Renegade, smuggler, gun-for-hire, former Captain of the *Renegade Star*, and the most wanted man in the galaxy.

Abigail Pryar (Abby) : Kidnapper, assassin, former nun, and Jace's second-in-command. Abigail risked her life in order to rescue the albino child Lex from a Union laboratory, inciting a series of events that would lead her to encountering Jace on Taurus Station. She now helms the *Galactic Dawn* on a recruitment operation in the Deadlands, searching for new colonists to bring to Earth.

. . .

Frederick Tabernacle (Freddie) : Former priest and scholar. Frederick is an expert on the writings of Dr. Darius Clare, the founder of the Church of the Homeworld. Despite his obvious fear and anxiety under pressure, Freddie is consistently reliable in the face of danger, willing to do anything for the sake of his friends and allies.

Octavia Brie : Assistant archaeologist, brilliant pilot, combat expert, and former Union medic, Octavia remains an invaluable asset in the mission to rebuild Earth. After being shot by Fratley Oxanos, Octavia lost the use of her legs and believed she would never be able to walk again. That is, until the crew discovered *Titan* and restored power to its medical bay. When not on the job, Octavia can be found with her colleague and close friend, Dr. Hitchens, though the true nature of their relationship remains somewhat ambiguous.

Dr. Thadius Hitchens (The Professor) : Archaeologist with a focus on Ancient Earth Theory. After the discovery of a group of albino colonists, Hitchens has turned his focus to teaching. He remains optimistic and jolly, no matter the situation, and is always looking to the future.

. . .

Alphonse Malloy (Al) : Former Union Constable and spy, expert military strategist, and stoic thinker. During his time at the Red Tower—the Constable intelligence center —Alphonse discovered detailed information on the experiments that were being performed on Lex. Appalled at what he had found, Alphonse disguised himself as a soldier on a ship that had been tasked with pursuing the *Renegade Star*, allowing him to ultimately encounter Jace Hughes. After saving Lex and proving his loyalty, Alphonse has become a valued member of the crew and a trusted ally in the fight to rebuild Earth.

Dr. MaryAnn Dressler : A former Union scientist on Priscilla, Dressler was kidnapped by Jace Hughes when they stole a Tritium Core for *Titan*. While she was initially highly critical of Jace, she has since reversed her stance, especially after witnessing his protective loyalty for Lex and the other colonists. Always analytical and logical in her approach, she remains distant from most of the crew, the only exception being Alphonse Malloy, whom she has grown quite fond of in recent weeks.

Lex : Discovered in a small pod when she was just an infant, Lex spent most of her life in a Union lab, due to her unique physiology and strange tattoos. The Union correctly believed that Lex held the key to rediscovering the lost homeworld known as Earth. Due to her Eternal ancestry, Lex possesses advanced healing, a greatly extended lifespan, albino skin, white hair, and blue eyes. As far as she or anyone else knows, Lex is truly the last of her kind, being the only pureblood Eternal known to exist. Despite this, Lex remains cheerful, often shining a light in an otherwise dark or dire situation.

Bolin Abernathy : A former scrap dealer, he and his daughter were rescued by the crew after being kidnapped by the Sarkonians. Bolin is a skilled pilot and trusted friend to anyone who would have him.

Karin Braid : A young but highly capable leader. Karin's mother Lucia taught her everything she knows. She and her people are descendants of a group of Eternals, though they do not possess all of their original abilities, such as immortality. Having spent a great deal of time with the Cognitive Janus, Karin is well-versed in ancient technology and remains a highly effective engineer, should the need arise.

Lucia : Over a century old, Lucia is still highly capable and one of the best hand-to-hand fighters on *Titan*. Her expertise with a staff makes her a valued asset on any mission.

. . .

Josef (Jo) : Karin's father. He spent years living in a cave, far from his family, hoping to find a Tritium core to save his people. After so long in isolation, Josef has chosen to embrace his new life on Verdun, spending as much time with his friends and family as possible.

Admiral-General Marcus Brigham (deceased) : The former leader of the Union fleet tasked with hunting down the *Renegade Star* and capturing Lex. He was killed by Jace in one-on-one combat. Upon his death, he promised Jace that the Union would never stop hunting him, no matter how far he ran.

Cognitives

Athena : The Cognitive in charge of *Titan*, a seed colony moon-like ship. Originally from Earth, Athena is a fully sentient intelligence over two thousand years old. Using hard light technology, Athena can manifest a body in any room on *Titan*, often popping in out of nowhere, surprising the crew. Years ago, when *Titan*'s Tritium core failed, Athena sent her crew out into space to colonize the stars. In time, they forgot about *Titan* and the Cognitive who lived there, but Athena did not forget. She waited, remaining in low power, until the day she received a signal from Earth.

The transmission said only one thing: "Earth is restored. Initiate Project Reclamation." With that, she attempted to contact the descendants of her former crew, but no one responded. After decades of unanswered transmissions, Athena decided to awaken the only remaining crew member, a young Eternal infant who had been left behind and discarded by the other humans—a girl who would grow to be called Lex. Athena sent the child away, still asleep, and hoped that whoever found her would follow the trail back to *Titan*.

Sigmond (Siggy) : Originally, a standard artificial intelligence given to Jace upon his acquisition of the *Renegade Star*. After receiving a personality program and name, Sigmond became a valued asset and long-time companion to Jace. He was eventually given several additional upgrades by Athena, allowing him to become exceedingly more efficient and, shortly thereafter, caused him to show signs of cognition. During the final confrontation with the Cognitive Hephaestus, Sigmond sacrificed himself to save Jace and the rest of the crew. At this time, he was believed to be lost forever. Shortly thereafter, however, Sigmond reappeared on *Titan*, manifesting himself before Jace as a fully realized Cognitive whose appearance was unlike any other.

. . .

Janus (deceased): The Cognitive in charge of Karin and Lucia's former home. He was originally created to oversee three facilities on the same planet, each with its own distinct assignment. After the facilities were overrun by an outbreak of Boneclaws (genetically modified Eternals), Janus lost all contact with Earth. He was left with only a few thousand survivors, whose lives became his only priority. It wasn't until the arrival of the Union that Janus lost his life, defending the colonists during the evacuation to *Titan*. His final request was for Jace to look after his people and defend them against those who mean to use them. It is a request that has stayed with Jace, always in the back of his mind. After his death, Athena was able to salvage part of Janus's shell, which she gave to Sigmond in order to give him additional functionality. This was the beginning of Sigmond's Cognitive evolution.

Algaia (deceased): The Cognitive in charge of Tiche and several facilities across Earth space. She was killed and her shell absorbed by Hephaestus, granting him access to Algaia's supply depots.

Hephaestus (deceased): The Cognitive in charge of the defense network and the drone factories. After two thousand years, Hephaestus is a shadow of his former self. His mind has deteriorated so much that he relies entirely on protocol, defending the Earth from all Transient vessels. After encountering *Titan*, Hephaestus shows aggression towards the ship, ultimately mounting a major assault against Jace and his crew. Thanks to the efforts of an upgraded artificial intelligence known as Sigmond, Hephaestus and his data storage Capsules are permanently destroyed.

Other Terms

Eternals : Advanced humans who have been genetically modified with advanced healing and extremely long lifespans. After a few centuries, an additional mutation caused the Eternals to develop albino features, giving them a distinct appearance. They are responsible for most of Earth's advanced technology, including the seed colony ships, such as *Titan*, as well as Tritium cores, slipspace drives, and Cognitives.

Transients : Normal humans who do not possess the Eternal gene. After Eternals arose on Earth, Transient humans were delegated to the lower class, unable to accumulate wealth or obtain high-level positions in either business or politics. This stagnation led to a rebellion in which the Transients demanded equal opportunity. To satisfy this need, the Eternals offered them a deal: venture out into the far-flung reaches of the galaxy and colonize distant worlds, taking their lives into their own hands. The Transients agreed, and so began the greatest mass exodus in Earth's history.

Slipspace : A dimension beneath our own in which faster-than-light travel is possible. While it is not fully understood, many theorize that slipspace tunnels are in a constant state of nuclear fusion and fission, destroying and creating atoms simultaneously at all times. It was believed that slip tunnels were a naturally occurring phenomenon, but this is incorrect. In truth, the slip tunnel network was created by ancient ships from Earth as they expanded across the galaxy. While some tunnels collapsed over time, many remained to this day, providing modern ships with a faster-than-light means of transportation. Since modern ships cannot create their own tunnels, they must continue to rely on the existing network to travel. *Titan* is the only known ship capable of forming new tunnels.

Slip Gap Point (S.G. Point) : The location between tunnels (i.e. the space between two tunnel entrances). Often the location of colonies and refueling stations, they serve as the intergalactic road stops of the slip tunnel network. While the busier S.G. Points are often heavily policed, the less active locations remain somewhat dangerous due to frequent attacks and surprise raids.

Turn-key : A special communications device created by the Eternals. Only those with the appropriate tattoos can operate them.

The Sarkonian Empire : A smaller, but still capable collection of planets. Located on the opposite side of the Deadlands from the Union, the Sarkonians are known to claim planets randomly and without warning. Recently, they struck a deal with the Union for the promise of more territory, should they deliver the *Renegade Star*.

The Union : The most powerful military force known to exist, the Union has control over dozens of star systems. They remain in pursuit of *Titan*, hoping to reacquire Lex so that they might use her genes to enhance their own soldiers. They claim to do this to protect their borders and their people, but all past actions show an empire whose only goal has been territorial expansion.

Earth : Often believed to be a myth, Earth is said to be the original cradle of humanity, home to lost, unparalleled technology, the likes of which have not been seen in nearly two thousand years. Unfortunately, not much is known about Earth's history after the Great Transient Exodus, resulting in a massive gap in information, but that hasn't stopped the Union from sending every available ship to find it. At the same time, Jace Hughes and his crew are determined to get there first to keep whatever awaits them out of the hands of their enemy.

Verdun : The first and only colony on Earth, built and occupied by Jace and his companions. It rests atop an elevated city, which is supported by heavy scaffolding. Not much is known about these platforms, except that they are the last remaining evidence of technology from a lost civilization. It is believed that these cities once housed the Eternals so that the Earth could be terraformed below them, though this remains only a theory.

1

I STOOD on the edge of Verdun, a city located high above the Earth. The buildings were supported by heavy scaffolding—hundreds of seven-meter-thick metal pillars.

Today's skies were unusually clear, so the ground's reflective and sparkling surface shined with absolute clarity. This was all due to the ongoing terraforming process, which continued the same way it had since the day our people first arrived.

It had been a month since *Titan* had found its way to this place, bringing three hundred colonists with it. Each of us had been in desperate need of a home, so much that we could hardly wait to step foot on fresh soil. We had expected to find a world rich with life and opportunity. Instead, we had discovered our new home was still under construction.

But that hadn't stopped us from packing our bags and moving in.

Not remotely.

So far, we'd managed to bring just about everyone from *Titan* down to Verdun. A few dozen personnel had remained on the artificial moon to continue its day-to-day operations, but for the most part, our people had taken to their new home with great satisfaction.

There was no shortage of eagerness or hard work in this place. Flawed as the prize might be, it was still ours, and we would keep it right.

"Mr. Hughes!" called a voice from behind me, near one of the buildings we'd converted into living quarters. I turned to see Lex waving as she walked towards me, holding a basket of freshly picked fruit under her arm. She had a bright smile on her pale face, her porcelain hair blowing in the wind.

"What do you have there, Lex?" I asked.

"Some fresh deki," she told me, tilting the basket so I could see. "Want one?"

I eyed the pink and red fruit, considering the girl's offer. "What's the catch?" I asked, crossing my arms and raising my brow so she'd know I was serious. "I'm skeptical."

"No catch," she said with a giggle.

"Oh?" I asked, feigning surprise. "Well, aren't you a generous gal." I snatched up a piece of deki and bit into the crisp skin. We'd chosen to plant this crop first, and it had taken quickly to the climate.

Dressler's idea, I had been told. The woman might've been rude, but she knew how to do her research, which apparently included agricultural living. Hell if I knew the first thing about crop rotations or how much water to drown a deki plant in, but she took to it like she'd been raised in a garden.

I wiped the juice from my mouth as I chewed. "What do you say, Lex?"

"About what?" she asked curiously.

"Beats me, kid. I was asking you."

She laughed and rolled her eyes. "Mr. Hughes, you're silly today."

I smirked and tousled her hair, looking back to the horizon and then to the land beneath us. The air was crisp and clean, more than I was used to, even compared to other habitable worlds. I had to imagine it had something to do with the terraforming process that was still taking place. All these elevated cities, kilometers above the surface, each with a factory at its center, producing atmosphere.

Athena told me this was due to the loss of the planet's magnetic field. The working theory was that the core had stopped turning at some point, probably long ago, so the Eternals—the former residents of this place—built themselves a network of factories all across the globe, hoping to remake the planet.

That was all speculation. None of us really knew what any of this was for or why the Eternals had chosen to do what they did. Hell, they weren't around to ask, so all we could do was look at the evidence and give our best guess.

I hated speculation, though, especially from a distance. The only way we were going to get answers about this place would be to get down there and start looking.

That wasn't to say that we hadn't done a little of that already. Abigail and I had led a team to check the local area beneath this city. We'd also landed on several other cities at different points around the planet, but the results were mixed, and priorities demanded our attention elsewhere, such as establishing a proper colony, growing food, clearing out some living space for our people, and making sure our newly acquired defense network remained operational.

"Sir," said a voice in my ear. "If you'll pardon the interruption."

Speak of the devil, I thought, then touched the comm. "What's up, Siggy?"

"You requested to know when Ms. Pryar arrived," he informed me.

I smiled at the name. "She's back already, is she?" I asked.

"The *Galactic Dawn* has entered the final slip tunnel towards Earth. Ms. Pryar wanted me to let you know she'll meet you at the loading dock once her ship arrives."

I glanced down at Lex. "Looks like Abigail's almost back."

"Really?" asked Lex, her eyes suddenly wide with excitement.

"What's the ETA, Siggy?" I asked.

"Three hours, sir."

"Won't be long," I said to Lex.

The little girl grinned. "I'm going to show her the garden right away! Wait until she sees all the things we grew."

"I'm sure she'll love them, kid," I said. "Siggy, let me know when she's ready to unload those new colonists."

"Of course, sir," answered Sigmond.

After procuring the *Galactic Dawn* from the Union, I had asked the maintenance crews to recover the ship and outfit her with new armaments, since we'd blown most of the weapons off its hull in the last fight. Thanks to Sigmond—who now had full access to a fleet of drones and several manufacturing stations—getting the parts we needed was easier than it normally would've been.

Of course, the ship wasn't exactly the same. The guns were now significantly stronger, made from old Earth tech, like the strike ships on *Titan*. This increased the *Dawn*'s overall firepower by nearly fivefold. Not a bad improvement, if you asked me.

I tapped my comm again. "Siggy, where's Octavia right now? She still out with Alphonse and Bolin?"

"Yes, sir," said the Cognitive. "At this exact moment, they are flying over a continent formally named Australia. Shall I have them recalled?"

"No, that's fine," I said. "Just tell them the *Galactic Dawn* is almost here."

I had ordered our squads to begin fly-overs of all the different cities, hoping to find something that might not necessarily show up on orbital scans. So far, nothing had come of it, but I was hopeful that if we continued, we'd eventually find a clue. I just didn't think it would take this long.

"Understood," said Sigmond. "They should return by this afternoon."

I glanced behind me at the garden and the other colonists. Hitchens stood under the shade of a nearby apartment building, wiping his forehead with a small towel before taking a drink from his canteen. He'd lost some weight in recent weeks, eager to work whenever we'd let him. Aside from running the school, he spent time in the garden or helping to clear and organize debris from the other buildings. We had so much work to do, even after all this time, and I anticipated there would be no shortage of it in the future.

Building a world wasn't easy business, but when it was over, we'd have a real home, safe from all those who would do us harm.

Freedom, I had found, was a powerful motivator.

"I WANT this building cleared by the end of the week," I told my renovations team. We were standing in the central atrium on the first floor, which had already been cleared and wiped down earlier in the day.

"That soon?" asked Billins, balking a little at the notion. "It took eight days to do the last one."

I motioned at the two new crew members I had assigned to this team. "You've got the extra hands. They should be enough to cut your time by a day, at least."

He nodded. "Yes, sir."

The team dispersed shortly, each of them splitting into groups of two and taking the neighboring rooms. I smiled at the sight, but especially Billins, who had done well in the short time he'd been with us.

"The sergeant seems to be adapting well," observed Sigmond, cutting into my thoughts. His statement surprised me with how perceptive it was, although I knew it shouldn't. Even back when he was an A.I., Siggy always had a way of getting inside my head.

"Not bad for a Union lackey," I said, keeping my voice low.

"His recent evaluation is quite positive," informed Sigmond.

"I saw," I said, leaning against the wall. "Seems a far cry from the fool we met on the *Dawn*. I was surprised he wanted to stay behind, what with me almost getting him killed."

"It has been said that a shared traumatic event can bond people," postulated Sigmond. "Perhaps he feels a connection to you and the others."

I thought back to the conversation I'd had with Billins about the prospect of returning to the Union. It was right after we had defeated Brigham and seized the *Galactic Dawn*.

He could've left with the other cruisers—probably gotten a pay raise out of it too, given his POW status. Instead, he'd chosen to stay, surprising us all. "I've never seen anyone do what you did," Billins had told me. "You beat the Union, and no one does that. Not even the Sarkonians. You did it all by yourselves, and I just think that's amazing. I figure if you can do something like that, maybe you can do more too. If you don't mind, I wanna be there when it happens, whatever that something is. I wanna see where you go next."

"If you come, you'll have to be one of us," I had said, standing with him next to the garden on *Titan*. "The Union might brand you as a traitor. It might be a problem for your family."

"I only have my cat Bean, and she's in my quarters on the *Galactic Dawn*," he'd told me. "Can I bring her too?"

I laughed as I replayed the conversation in my head, imagining the little black and white cat in Billins' arms. He'd brought her with him to the colony, even let the kids play with her from time to time. None of us treated him poorly, far as I knew, and he seemed eager to do his part, same as the rest.

It could have easily gone the other way.

"Captain!" called a voice from outside.

"That sounds like Dr. Hitchens," said Sigmond.

I eased off the wall and walked to the front door. The sun hit me with momentary blindness as my eyes adjusted to a cloudless sky. "What is it, Hitchens?" I asked, squinting.

The jolly archeologist waddled up to the nearby stairs, sweat beading down his cheeks. "I was hoping to inquire with you, regarding the appropriation of a classroom for the children. The room we're currently occupying is a little too small for our needs. I can't imagine how cramped it will become once the new families arrive this afternoon."

I sighed. "I'll see what I can do, Prof."

"Thank you, Captain," said Hitchens, a wide grin on his face. "You have no idea how happy this will make the children."

I leaned inside the building. "Billins!" I barked.

"Yes, sir!" he called, his voice echoing through the atrium. The boy came running, fumbling with a mop as he halted to a stop in front of me. "W-what's wrong? Is everything all right?"

"Everything's fine, Billins," I assured him. "I need you to focus on clearing out the largest room on this floor. Help Hitchens here move whatever equipment he needs into it."

"Equipment?" asked Billins, looking at Hitchens.

"Just a few dozen tables and chairs. Oh, and possibly some lab instruments for the students." He chuckled. "The children do enjoy their projects."

"You can handle this, right?" I asked, raising my brow. "If not, I can always ask someone else."

Billins stiffened. "O-of course, sir! Leave it to me."

I nodded then motioned for him to get back to it. He bustled off to the other room, calling the rest of his team to refocus their efforts.

"I must say, Captain, that boy is as eager as they come," observed Hitchens. "Although we don't necessarily need the room right this moment. There's no reason to rush if he has other work to do."

"He's trying to prove himself," I explained. "I figure I'll let him do just that."

"Ah, I see," said Hitchens. "In that case, by all means. The children will be excited to have a larger area to study in."

Hitchens gave me a courteous nod and proceeded to the garden across the street, joining a handful of others as they harvested a batch of deki fruit.

Verdun, the first colony in the new world, was finally coming into its own. "Let me help you with some of that," I called after Hitchens as he picked up one of the baskets.

The archeologist smiled. "Thank you, Captain. Another set of hands certainly wouldn't hurt."

THE *GALACTIC DAWN* arrived in orbit shortly after Hitchens and I finished up with the harvest. Sigmond informed me that he'd already arranged to have a shuttle take me there, to which I quickly agreed.

I walked through the middle of the city, looking over the buildings along the street. Most of them were empty, waiting for us to clean and refit them. Alphonse and I had already chosen which would be the dorms and which would be used for other services, such as medical, storage, and recreational centers. Truth of the matter was that we'd only managed to clear about ten percent of the city, leaving most of it untouched. Limited manpower would do that.

But the new colonists were coming soon, and that meant a fresh workforce ready to build. In a few years, maybe less, we'd have this entire city occupied and running. Maybe it wouldn't be perfect—nothing ever is—but I'd make absolutely sure it worked.

There weren't many dangers on this planet, at least that we'd been able to find. The only threat seemed to be the little machines located on the planet's surface—automated robots that came and went, and whose purpose seemed to be a total mystery. They resembled bottom-feeder shellfish, like something you might find in the deep ocean, consuming the waste of other animals.

Because of this, many of the colonists had taken to calling them trilobites, based on one of the entries in *Titan*'s Old Earth historical database.

Unlike their namesake, these trilobites seemed to have a unique purpose.

Shortly after discovering them, we dropped a metal

crate nearby, just to see what would happen. To our surprise, the machines swarmed the box, quickly liquifying the metal. From there, they absorbed it into their bodies and retreated underground.

I was going to leave them alone after that, at least until we understood more about them. That was when the lookout reported seeing them at the base of the city, right next to the lower scaffolding.

The trilobites did nothing at first. They simply sat there, never leaving, never doing much of anything. After seeing what they'd done to our crate, I decided to have them put down.

The following morning, Bolin and a team of our best sharpshooters rained a hailstorm of bullets down on the machines until they were completely immobilized.

I expected that to be the end of it, but I was wrong.

More machines came as soon as we killed the others. They latched on to their dead brothers and, just as they had done to the crate, liquified their remains before returning into the ground again. Within the hour, another group had emerged, taking up position near the scaffolding, and waiting.

We tried killing them a few more times, but it was always the same. Shoot a trilobite and another liquified it, taking its place. There seemed to be no end to them.

I was beginning to wonder what was going through their little heads and why they'd taken a liking to our city, but no others. What had possessed them to gather together down there? Was something controlling them?

They remained at the base of the scaffolding every hour of every day, never leaving except for a few minutes after we killed them. I didn't fully understand what they were or why they were there—only that this was a problem I needed to fix. I only had to figure out how.

That was why I'd sent Alphonse and Octavia out on their own. Each and every day for the last two weeks, those two had been searching for answers, and I expected they'd find something soon. If they didn't, then the strike ships I had scouring the solar system for anything with a Sarkonian or Union signature would do the trick. One way or another, we'd find out who or what was responsible.

I approached the shuttle on the landing pad and climbed inside, strapping into the pilot's chair. I touched the control pad, ordering the ship to prime its engines.

When I did, a hologram appeared on the dash. "Good afternoon, Captain Hughes," said Athena, blinking her artificial blue eyes. "Taking a visit to the *Galactic Dawn*?"

"You know it," I answered. "What can I do you for, Athena?"

She smiled. "I was hoping to place a request, if you have the time to hear it."

"I've got thirty minutes before I dock," I said, lifting the ship off the pad. "Let's hear it."

"If you could spare the engineers, it would please me

very much to increase the number of holo emitters on Verdun."

"Isn't this something Karin and Dressler are supposed to be handling?" I asked. "Why are you asking me?"

"They're currently occupied with more pressing concerns, I'm afraid. However, I believe you have thirteen capable engineers arriving today with sufficient educational backgrounds who could—"

"Athena," I interjected, cocking my brow at the hologram. "Are you already trying to poach our new recruits?"

"Guilty as charged, Captain," said the Cognitive. "I hope you'll pardon my ambition. With everyone on the surface, I feel rather isolated here."

"Isolated? Didn't you spend close to two thousand years alone before we showed up?"

"I did, but now I find myself longing for the company," she admitted. "I suppose I've grown used to it lately. I apologize for my selfish request, Captain."

I chuckled. "I'll see what I can do, Athena."

"That is all I ask," she said, instantly disappearing from the dash.

In her place, a holo readout of the system appeared, indicating my position as well as the *Galactic Dawn*'s. I had plenty of time before I arrived, which meant I could either rest my eyes or catch up on some reading.

Alphonse, Hitchens, and Dressler had all sent me packets of work logs, notes, and a shitload of requests. Athena wasn't the only one who wanted me to assign her some new personnel. It seemed like every single department head was in dire need of more recruits.

I decided to ignore all of that for right now, since I hadn't even met the new arrivals yet. Instead, I leaned back in my seat and stared out the window, watching as the blue sky faded into black as I left the atmosphere. Below, I could still see Verdun, located on one of many identical elevated cities that were spread across the globe.

2

I STEPPED off the loading platform and onto the landing bay of the *Galactic Dawn*. Immediately, I was met by a sea of people—over a hundred future colonists scurrying about the deck, most of their faces reflecting both excitement and uncertainty. It was a look that I had grown accustomed to during my time traveling the stars. I'd seen countless refugees, especially in the Deadlands, and they always had that same look in their eyes.

You could almost feel the uncertainty and nervousness in the air. None of these people truly knew what to expect once they arrived on Earth. All they understood was what we'd told them, which wasn't much—only that they would be part of the first colony on a rediscovered Earth, a planet that, as it turned out, was actually real and not just a story in a children's book. They had, of course, needed proof, and we'd provided it through censored videos and images, but it didn't take much to convince them to come. These were displaced people under fire from two empires, all of them living in constant fear of war.

We'd specifically chosen worlds like theirs, near the Union and Sarkonian borders, because of that fear. These were worlds on the verge of being conquered, and the people living on them knew it. They just couldn't do anything about it.

The Union and Sarkonian Empire had invaded and claimed multiple systems over the last decade, but increasingly so in recent months. The Deadlands were shrinking a little more with each passing week, giving its residents more cause to flee, pushing them deeper and deeper into the neutral territory between empires.

But the Deadlands wouldn't last forever. It wouldn't take long before the Union and the Sarkonians swallowed them all up, dividing everything between them. There would be no more free worlds. There would only be the conquered.

That was where we came in. The Earth's territory contained several habitable worlds with bountiful resources, each one ready for colonization. Most of all, they had our protection—a fleet of drones and ships to guard our borders. The Union wouldn't be able to touch these people—not after we'd taken out most of their ships and sent them packing. With Sigmond producing more defense drones every day, not to mention a newly outfitted *Galactic*

Dawn and *Titan*, we had everything we needed to ensure our new friends' survival.

Of course, the Deadlands was notorious for its share of criminals—all manner of unsavory sorts, such as murderers, thieves, and all the nasties in between. But there were good folks there too. People who only wanted to make an honest living and do right by themselves and their kin. I wagered they deserved a chance to see it done, even if it was on the other side of the galaxy, on a world they didn't know.

Time would tell if the gamble we made would pay off, if this blooming colony of ours would prosper and become what we wanted it to be, or if Brigham's words to me would be proven right, and the whole enterprise would come crashing down, burying me in the process.

Looking out across the bay at all the many faces who had come so far with so little, I couldn't help but feel a little more optimistic.

"Look!" exclaimed someone from the crowd. "That's Captain Hughes!"

A handful of refugees approached me. "The Renegade?" asked one of them. "I heard he was taller than that. Are you sure that's him?"

"He looks just like his wanted poster," exclaimed a teenager.

They went silent, staring at me with slack-jawed expressions. The whole scene unnerved me, but thankfully, all of that was soon broken by a voice laughing from beyond the crowd.

"Ah, yes. There he is," said Lucia, parting the colonists as she walked casually in my direction. She glanced sideways at the nearby onlookers, bearing an annoyed expression. "You certainly took your time, boy."

"Don't start with me, old woman," I said.

She eyed me for a moment then smirked and presented her hand. I took it, and we shook. "Nice to see you again."

I nodded. "Two weeks is too long."

She motioned for me to return with her, towards the elevators on the other side of the bay. We walked through the crowd, each of the colonists turning as we passed, their eyes transfixed on us.

"Tell me something," I said, once we'd put some space between us and the crowd.

"You're wondering about the mob," she said, laughing. "It seems our story has spread far. Tales of your exploits are all over the Deadlands now." She stepped up to the elevator and scanned her access card, opening the doors. We both stepped inside. "Captain Jace Hughes—the Renegade, they're calling you."

"That's what I am," I said casually.

She shook her head. "You were *a* Renegade, but now you're *the* Renegade. There is a difference. Perhaps a bit dramatic, but what do I know? I'm just an old woman raised in an ice cave."

I peered out of the lift as the doors closed, locking eyes

with the crowd as they watched me from afar. "Those people don't know what they're talking about."

"They know enough," she answered. "Talk of your match with Brigham has spread like an avalanche."

I scoffed. "They know what you tell them or what they hear. None of them were there. The real battle was fought in orbit, decided by Siggy and the rest of the fleet. They should be hailing Octavia, Bolin, or Alphonse. They—"

She raised her finger a few centimeters from my face. "Doesn't matter. You can't stop the flow of gossip." She snickered. "Those people know you didn't do this alone, but they know you did enough. You're the man who defied two empires, rediscovered Earth, and built himself an army. Face it, boy. Your story's bigger than you now."

I stared at the doors until they opened, saying nothing. The whole thing made me uncomfortable, and I aimed to put a stop to the so-called gossip as soon as I had the chance. For now, though, I had other priorities, such as the status of this ship and the people waiting in its landing bay. We'd have to organize them, deploy them, and assign every capable man, woman, and child with a task that needed doing.

Lucia and I walked quietly to the bridge, an air of silence in the corridor. I recalled when I first infiltrated this place and how it bustled with Union activity. All of that noise was gone, replaced by a somber stillness. It was almost eerie, like a ghost ship, but without the corpses.

As the doors opened and we stepped inside the bridge, I

was met by the image of the Earth across a large screen against the forward wall. I recalled the first time I'd seen this world, back when Freddie had shown it to me on the *Renegade Star*. It was so green and blue, with some of the largest continents I'd ever seen on a class-M planet.

The reality was so much different, a brown and empty world with no vegetation or animals to speak of. Nothing but oceans of empty water and continents of dead land.

Any other group might see this and be discouraged, but not my people. Earth's new colonists were eager to build and make the planet ready. They saw the work it needed and believed they could see it done. None of us knew the full extent of what that work might entail, or if the dream of Earth might ever truly be realized, but maybe that was for the best. It wasn't always the goal that mattered, but the journey to see it done that made the difference. We would keep trying to make a life, and if we were lucky, maybe one day we'd succeed.

A dozen hand-picked personnel scurried around the bridge, hard at work coordinating what was about to be their second mission—another recruitment job to the Deadlands. This would be the second set of colonists—or third, if you included the original group. Those worlds had already been mapped out weeks ago by Sigmond and Alphonse, chosen because of their proximity to the Union or Sarkonian borders. That was where tensions would be at their strongest, which meant they would be the most eager to leave. A message had already been sent across the gal-net, informing every resident of our invitation. None of us knew how many people would opt to join us or how much resistance we might encounter, but we were hopeful. That was all a part of the risk, and it was one I had entrusted to Abigail, above all others.

Thankfully, we'd chosen the very best personnel from among Lucia's team—individuals with a natural talent for inflicting pain. Of course, few of them compared to the woman standing at the center of the bridge, hands behind her back. Her brownish-blonde hair remained a stark contrast to the rest of the albino crew, and I knew it far too well.

Abigail turned to look at me, an immediate smile etched across her beautiful face. "Jace!" she called, and I knew right away that she was just as happy to see me as I was to see her.

I returned the smile, but only for a second. Now that we were in charge of an army, not to mention all of those colonists on the lower decks, we couldn't let ourselves get carried away by affection.

Not right now anyway.

No, based on the hungry expression she was giving me, I gave it twenty minutes before we ended up in either her quarters or one of the nearby side offices. In any case, it didn't much matter to me.

I was never one for particulars.

"Lucia here tells me everything went pretty well," I said.

"She did?" asked Abigail, shooting a quick glance at the old woman.

Lucia cocked her brow. "Nobody died."

"What does that mean?" I asked. "Did something happen?"

Lucia rolled her eyes and turned around. "You can tell him if you want," she said, walking to the exit door. "I have other matters that need my attention."

She proceeded to leave, apparently uninterested in the conversation she knew we were about to have. "What the hell is she talking about?" I asked Abigail.

"It's not a big deal, Jace," she answered. "We had to deal with some miscreants, that's all."

"Miscreants?" I asked.

She said nothing, so I simply stared at her, waiting for more answers. After a few moments, she finally sighed and continued. "Fine. We were ambushed on the ground by a Union assault squad. Six of them, but—"

"An assault squad?!" I snapped, causing several of the crew to look at me.

Abigail waved her hand at them then lowered her voice. "We handled it. Don't worry. Those personal shields took most of the damage."

"Most?" I asked, holding on to the word.

"They took us by surprise, so not everyone had time to activate their shield. Karin took a hit in the shoulder, but she's fine. The med pod we brought had her healed in a matter of hours."

"Gods, Abby," I muttered. "Why didn't you order everyone to keep their shields up?"

She gave me a look, but I ignored it.

"Well?" I asked.

"Because it happened on the ship," she finally admitted.

"On the *Dawn*?" I asked.

She nodded. "Operatives posing as civilians."

I let out a long sigh, crossing my arms as I tried to imagine how something like that could even happen. "Fake IDs? Or were they stowaways?"

"Fakes, and good ones too," she said. "I sent them to Sigmond as soon as we reached Abaddon and he tells me he can create a better authentication tool for future runs. We shouldn't encounter this problem again."

"I want your security team doubled," I said without hesitation.

"That's really not necessary, Jace."

"I don't give a damn what's necessary. I've got a fleet of drones between the Earth and the Union, but only the hull of this ship to protect all of you when you're out there. We shouldn't underestimate the Union, Abby."

She leaned towards me and smiled. "I see what's going on here. You're concerned about my well-being."

I stayed rigid. "You know damn well that I am."

She paused a few centimeters from my chest, nudging me with her palm, then motioned with her eyes to the nearby office, inviting me. "Prove it."

3

"Gods, I needed that," said Abigail, lying bare-chested on the conference table. She ran her fingers down my chest, tickling me in the process.

I fidgeted, nudging the barrel of my pistol against my naked ass. I pushed the gun away so it wasn't digging into my side anymore then turned to look at Abby. "Not a bad welcome home, I'd say."

"Is that what you say?" she asked.

"I might. That all depends on what else we get up to," I said, giving her a knowing smile. "Care for another?"

Abigail opened her mouth to answer but paused at the sound of a bell, followed by three knocks. "Ma'am?" called the voice from the other side of the door. "We have a bit of a situation."

"What kind of situation?" I yelled in return.

Abigail leapt off the table and tossed her shirt back on, causing me to groan. "They wouldn't be calling me if it wasn't important," she explained.

"There's been an incident in one of the bays involving two colonists," explained the voice.

Abigail hurried over to the door, buttoning her shirt and running her fingers through her hair. After a quick second, she gave up on looking entirely professional and proceeded to open the door.

An albino woman stood there, stepping back momentarily when she saw Abigail. "Oh, excuse me. I know you asked not to be disturbed, but—" The woman's eyes drifted over to me and my naked ass on the table. I gave her a grin and a quick wave, and she awkwardly returned it. "—the situation is escalating," she continued, looking back at Abigail. "The security team has already been dispatched and they are handling the situation, but the nature of it seemed to require elevation."

"How's that?" Asked Abigail.

"The colonist responsible for the confrontation was attempting to steal supplies from one of the families. He managed to get his hands on a knife and was using it to threaten the family."

"Didn't you scan these people before they boarded?" I asked, reaching for my pants.

The woman nodded. "Yes, sir. Our security team personally scanned every individual that boarded the ship.

We intend to investigate where he acquired the weapon as soon as we have the opportunity."

"I want that colonist in an interrogation room right away," ordered Abigail.

"Yes, ma'am," said the soldier. "I'll have him brought to the brig right away for questioning. Shall I relay this information to Lucia so that she can begin?"

"Lucia?" I asked, buckling my belt. I reached down and picked up my shirt. "You put her in a cell with a man, she's bound to kill him. At the very least, break a bone or two. Best make sure someone goes in there with her. I'm not a fan of good cop, bad cop, so it might do you well to send someone else."

“Good point,” conceded Abby. “I suppose I can handle this one myself.”

There was a light click in my ear, followed by a familiar voice. "Sir, if you'll pardon the interruption. Miss Brie has returned from her scouting efforts, along with Mr. Malloy. I believe the data they collected calls for your eyes, if you have a moment."

"Now ain’t a good time, pal," I said, strapping on my holster.

Abigail looked at me.

I pointed to my ear. “Just Siggy.”

“It's okay,” she assured me. “If you have something to do, I can take it from here."

"I know you can. I just figured I could see you in action."

"I assure you, it won't be that entertaining," said Abigail.

"All the same," I said, securing my holster. "Let's hear what this so-called thief has to say."

I STOOD in the rear of a large oval-shaped room, watching Abigail as she repeated a question to the man in the cell. "What were you thinking?"

"I-I don't know!" exclaimed the man, whose name was apparently Trevor. "I just got this feeling like it might be my last chance to—" He paused, scratching his hands and shifting in his chair. "—to eat for a while. I d-dunno how to e-explain it. I j-just couldn't stop thinking about it."

Trevor fidgeted again in his seat, scratching his hands and then his neck. He was also blinking a lot, licking his lips, and his eyes were all over the room, unable to stay still. I couldn't see them from where I was standing, but I guessed his pupils were probably dilated to hell too.

Before Abigail could ask him something else, the door opened, and a woman walked in, carrying a pad. She handed it to Abigail, who read it and promptly returned the device. The woman took it—one of the albinos, of course, although she seemed a little more glammed up than the rest. Her hair had been fixed, and I thought I caught sight of some eyeliner and makeup. Very uncommon for Lucia's people. Then again, there was no telling what sort of fashion tips the crew had picked up during their time in the Deadlands.

The woman walked to the side of the door and stood at attention.

"Stay here for a moment, Mr. Parcelle," said Abby.

"O-okay, s-sure will," said Trevor.

She turned away and approached me, keeping her back to the prisoner's cell.

"Let me guess," I whispered to her. "He's on something."

"The toxicology report just came back," said Abigail, sighing as she spoke the words.

"What's his poison?" I asked.

"Milocliptinide," she answered. "I believe the street term is Sweet Pie."

I pulled my head back and dropped my jaw a little. "Since when do you know about drugs?"

She smiled and rolled her eyes. "You'd be surprised what I know."

I smirked. "I'm sure I would."

Abigail looked over her shoulder at Trevor. "He needs to detox, but we should have him clean in a few hours. This isn't our first case of drug use, although it certainly is for Milocliptinide."

"You've had other drug addicts?" I asked.

"A few, but none of them were violent. Trevor might be the first," she said.

"What are you going to do about it?"

She sighed. “From what I understand, paranoia is a side effect, along with short bursts of aggression.”

I didn’t say anything.

“But,” she continued, “we can’t let something like this go. He’ll need to be reprimanded.”

“What’s the punishment?” I asked.

“Hard labor in the field for a month,” she said. “Better to make him useful than a burden.”

“Not bad, Captain Pryar,” I said, smiling. “You might have a knack for this whole command thing.”

“Please,” she said, dismissing the compliment. “The next time this ship makes a recruitment run, you’re the one at the helm. I’d rather spend my time on the ground and under the sun.”

“You’d look good with a tan,” I told her.

She smirked. “Damn right I would.”

4

I FOUND myself back on the landing bay, stepping clear of the elevators, when someone yelled my name.

Freddie came running from the crowd, trying to get my attention. "Hey!" he called as he neared. "Captain, I heard you were onboard. Good to see you again!"

"I was starting to wonder where you were, Freddie," I said, giving him a quick once-over. "How's your new job working out?"

"It's good!" he exclaimed, apparently unable to hide his excitement. "Aside from a few problems, our first mission was a success."

"That's great," I said.

He smiled. "Thank you, but I'm eager to see the progress you've made on the colony. Would you mind if I joined you on the surface?"

"Are you trying to bum a ride with me?" I asked.

He hesitated, almost embarrassed. "Oh, I didn't mean to—"

"Cut the bullshit, Freddie, and tell me why you're asking," I interrupted.

"It's just that, well, we've been on this ship for days now and I could really use the reprieve." He looked around, almost suspiciously. "You understand, don't you?"

"Me?" I asked curiously. "Is that supposed to be some kind of joke?"

"A joke?" he repeated.

"Do you have any idea how much I'd prefer cruising in a starship to—" I paused. "—well, anything else?"

He didn't say anything.

"Besides, it hasn't been easy down there for anyone," I continued. "Even if I didn't enjoy living off the land, you know full well how infertile the whole damn planet is, and those elevated cities aren't exactly the most hospitable. We've had to cycle out two dozen crops just to get one that sticks, thanks to the temperature fluctuations."

"You finally managed to grow something?" he asked.

"Deki," I said. "Tart and sweet, once you break the skin, which is three centimeters, by the way. It's a far cry from—" I stopped, tilting my head. "Hold on. You still haven't answered my question. Why the hell are you trying to leave? And don't try to bullshit me, Fred. You should know by now that I can smell it."

He gulped. "O-okay, Captain. You're right. I'm just

trying to avoid somebody, that's all. It's nothing serious."

"Avoid?" I asked, crossing my arms. "Is someone giving you a hard time? Is it one of the colonists? Want that we should teach them a lesson?"

He waved his arms back and forth. "No, no!" he exclaimed. "Nothing like that!"

"Then what?" I asked.

"Uh," he muttered, cringing at the question. "Well, it's nobody. She's just—"

"She?" I asked, suddenly more interested in Freddie's babbling.

"J-just one of the soldiers we brought from Lucia's team. It doesn't matter, really, Captain."

"Well now, Freddie, I think I beg to differ," I said, crossing my arms. "What's this girl's name?"

"Frederick?" called a voice from the other side of the bay.

Freddie tensed up, looking over his shoulder at the far end, near the other elevators. "There she is!"

"Oh?" I asked.

"I heard she was looking for me," he said, more afraid than I'd seen him in some time. He grabbed my wrist. "Please, Captain!"

I raised my hand, but not all the way. "I think I'd like to meet this woman."

"N-no!" he stuttered.

"Why not? She seems nice," I argued. "And I wanna find out what her name is, since you won't say."

"It's Petra!" he blurted out.

"Petra, eh?" I asked, chewing on the name. "She sounds too good for you."

"But you don't know anything about her," he said.

I shook my head. "Doesn't matter. If she's a woman, she's too good."

He frowned in defeat.

I reached into my pocket and retrieved the shield Abigail had given me.

"What's that for?" asked Freddie.

I smacked the device on my shoulder, activating it with the tap of a button. Instantly, I took on the appearance of an albino soldier—white hair, blue eyes, and pale skin, wearing the same uniform as the others. "Too many eyes on me when I landed," I explained.

"You don't like your new celebrity status?" asked Freddie.

"I'll talk to these people when all of us are on the ground and I don't have a list of other priorities to deal with."

Freddie nodded as we walked towards the crowd. Most of them ignored us, except to step out of the way, since I looked like a member of the crew and it was presumed that I had important business to attend to.

When we reached the airlock, I entered my access code to open the door, breaking the seal. "How many colonists did you bring us anyway?" I asked, glancing at Freddie.

"Didn't Abigail give you the report?" he asked.

"We got a little—" I paused. "—distracted. Just tell me."

"I think it's somewhere around two hundred," he said, but didn't seem entirely certain.

"Not a bad haul," I answered.

He nodded. "Abigail said the same—"

"Frederick!" yelled a voice from across the bay. It was a woman, albino, wearing a blue top and black pants. She locked eyes with us and waved, a fierce look in her eyes.

"Uh, oh," muttered Freddie.

I always had a hard time distinguishing the albinos when they were this far away, but as I continued to stare, I quickly realized it was the same woman I'd seen in the brig—the one who'd given Abigail that toxicology report. Apparently, I'd been spending time with Freddie's little girlfriend without even realizing it.

Small world.

"Frederick! Where are you going?!" shouted Petra.

I felt a hand on my bicep, tugging my sleeve. "I think we should go, Captain!"

The shield distorted from the interference of Freddie's hand, so I quickly shrugged him off. "Easy, man. What's the big deal? Are you really that terrified of a woman?"

"Frederick!" called Petra.

"Captain!" pleaded Freddie. He took a step back into the airlock.

I rolled my eyes. "Oh, all right." I smacked the back of his shoulder, shoving him further through the door. "But you owe me one, kid. And I want to know what the deal is with whatever the hell this is." I motioned to the closing airlock right as Petra arrived.

The woman banged on the wall with her fist, a hungry look in her eyes. I stayed near the door, raising my brow, then turned away and sat in the pilot's chair in the front. Freddie was already strapped in beside me, nervous sweat beads pouring down his forehead.

I reached to the dash and touched the control pad, activating the engines and detaching from the *Galactic Dawn* in one fluid motion. As we trailed off and away from the carrier ship, I heard Freddie breathe a long sigh of relief.

I looked at him, pausing to see if he was going to actually say anything or if I was gonna have to pull it out of him.

Thankfully, Freddie knew better than to make me ask. "I'm so sorry about that, Captain," he apologized. "This is so embarrassing. Please don't say anything to Abigail or the others about this. I'd rather nobody find out."

"I'll decide for myself once I hear what you did to that *poor* woman."

He frowned, bowing his head in shame. "Petra and I have been seeing each other for the past month."

I scoffed. "Seems to me like she was a little perturbed at you, Freddie. What the hell did you do?"

"Well, y-you see," he began, bumbling over his words. "She wants me to meet her family."

"Her family?" I chuckled. "Is that all?"

He waved his hands and shook his head. "It's not what you think. In their culture, getting introduced to the family is a big deal."

"How big?" I asked.

"It's something you do right before you get married," he explained.

The words hung in the air for a few seconds as I imagined Freddie standing in the middle of an aisle, dressed in a suit, waiting for his bride. When I added in the prospect of an albino father-in-law standing beside him with a weaponized staff in his hands, I couldn't help but have a nice, long laugh. "Freddie, you stupid bastard."

"Captain, I know!" he exclaimed, throwing his head into his hands, elbows on his knees. "I have no idea what to do! I care about Petra. Quite a bit, actually. She's beautiful and a gifted scientist. I just don't think I'm ready to do all of that."

"Sounds to me like you might not have much of a choice, pal."

A voice broke in on the comms, disrupting our conversation. "Captain, this is Octavia. Alphonse, Bolin, and I have returned to Verdun."

"I hear you, Octavia. I'm on my way back with Freddie," I answered.

"I trust I'm not interrupting anything," she said.

I glanced at Freddie. "No, we were just discussing poor life choices. Go ahead with whatever you've got."

"Well, we didn't find anything abnormal in grids 61, 62,

63, or 64," she explained. "However, because we still had another hour on the clock, we decided to go ahead and investigate grid 65."

"And?" I asked.

"*And*," she continued, "we found something."

I perked up then leaned forward. "I'm listening."

"You'll recall the trilobites?” she continued.

“What about them?" I asked.

"We spotted a trail of them, crawling through the cliffs, and we decided to follow them for as long as possible. At the end of it, we discovered something interesting."

"And what's that?" I asked.

"An opening," she said somewhat emphatically. "A massive chasm leading into the ground, undetectable by normal scans, with at least two hundred trilobites along its inner walls."

My eyes widened at the thought of such a place. "How's that possible? Why couldn't we see it from *Titan*?"

"I don't know," she admitted. "But I'd certainly like to find out."

I scratched the side of my jaw. "Meet me back at Verdun. I want the three of you ready to leave immediately."

"Let me guess," she responded. "You'd like to have yourself a look. See it up-close?"

"Wouldn't you?" I asked, cocking my brow. I turned to Freddie and cracked a half smile. "Seems like you got here just in time, Fred. Things just got a little more interesting."

5

I SAT inside the room that had recently been converted into my office, although it was really more like a collection of storage crates and equipment. I'd been using a table we had found during cleanup, and I was in no rush to replace it. I spent so little time here, I figured it hardly mattered. Aside from the Foxy Stardust bobblehead—which currently sat on my desk—everything in this room was expendable.

Alphonse, Octavia, and Freddie were already here, ready to discuss the situation involving the recent find. I was eager to get things underway, but I didn't want to do this without the rest of my team. That meant waiting for Abigail, Lucia, Dressler, and Karin to arrive, not to mention the two Cognitives.

"How long should we wait?" asked Octavia.

"Abigail and Dressler are on their way," said Alphonse. “I can’t speak for the others.”

I nodded. “As soon as they're here, we’ll brief everyone on your findings. I want that site secured by the end of the day.”

“Secured?” asked Freddie.

A flicker of gold light caught my eye as Sigmond appeared beside my desk. We had just recently installed a set of hard light emitters, giving both Athena and Sigmond the ability to come and go as they pleased. Before that, we had to use mobile emitters, which were less reliable and didn't allow for direct interaction with the local environment. That was what the Cognitives had claimed anyway.

If you asked me, I think they just liked making demands.

Sigmond smiled as his body quickly materialized. "Since receiving this information, Athena and I have been analyzing the terrain. We have several theories on its nature."

Another spark of light, this time blue, began to appear right next to Sigmond. “As well as the reason we could not detect it before today,” finished Athena.

“It sounds like you need more data,” said Octavia.

“An understatement,” replied Athena. “The pit appears to be quite deep, possibly several kilometers.”

“You can’t tell?” I asked.

“Something is disrupting our scans,” she answered. “An electromagnetic field possibly.”

"But you don't know," said Alphonse.

"Correct," she said.

The door opened and Dressler walked inside, along with Karin. "Good afternoon, everyone," addressed the doctor. She took an empty chair and brought it beside Alphonse. "I trust we haven't missed much."

Karin joined her, taking the last remaining chair.

"We were waiting for you," said Freddie.

"I appreciate that," she said.

"How long before Abigail and Lucia get here?" I asked, looking at Sigmond.

"They departed some time ago," he answered.

"Who departed?" asked a voice from the doorway. Abigail beamed a smile towards me, crossing her arms as she leaned against the wall. Lucia was right behind her, looking as stoic as ever.

"Eerie timing," remarked Octavia. "Were you waiting in the hall to make an entrance?"

"No, that was just luck," answered Abigail.

The two women came inside and shut the door, each of them remaining on their feet. "Let's go ahead and get started," I finally said, looking at Alphonse and Octavia. "Tell them everything you told me, and don't leave anything out."

THE BRIEFING WAS quick and to the point. Octavia explained what her team had found, laying out the day's events in chronological order, and then the conversation shifted to Athena's attempts to scan the interior of the chasm.

Unfortunately, after an hour of theories and explanations, we still knew very little. "The fact is, we won't fully comprehend what we're dealing with until we go there and investigate," said Alphonse.

"It's large enough to fit a handful of strike ships," said Octavia. "We could take a squad."

"Each ship can be configured to perform continuous proximity scans," said Athena. "Data collection should multiply with each additional ship."

"Hold on," said Freddie, pulling everyone's attention to him. "Are we actually sure we need to investigate this?"

"What do you mean?" asked Octavia.

"Well," he continued, scratching his ear. "If the planet is terraforming itself, maybe that hole is part of the process. If we interfere with it, we may cause a problem."

"That is a valid concern," agreed Athena. "However, without knowing the cause and purpose of the chasm, we cannot definitively state such a conclusion. It is, therefore, just as likely that the formation is a product of a failing system."

I leaned forward. "You think that hole isn't supposed to be there?"

"I do not know," admitted Athena. "There is so much

about this planet that I do not fully comprehend. It is but a shadow of the world I remember, and I would very much like to know why."

Bolin raised a finger. "I think this might be a good time to point out the trilobites gathering underneath the city too."

"What about them?" I asked.

"I meant to tell you, but a few more showed up this morning," he explained. "They're just sitting there, doing nothing, but it's concerning."

"And every time we shoot one, another pops up to take its place," said Karin.

Bolin nodded. "If they attack, we can probably take them all out, but more are bound to come, just like always."

Dressler nodded. "Bolin is correct. That chasm might give us information that could allow us to better understand the machines. It's worth investigating."

The idea that the chasm might hold answers had certainly grabbed my attention. I just wasn't sure about it being an accident or even a byproduct of some terraforming process. Considering how those trilobites beneath the city were acting, I was inclined to believe that someone was controlling them. Why else would a bunch of automated machines act so strangely? What reason did they have to gather together like that?

But if that was true, who were the people responsible?

The Union was one option, and I sure as hell wouldn't put this past them. Brigham had told me they wouldn't stop chasing us, and I had no reason to doubt him, but still. Abigail had stopped a squad of their thugs from boarding the *Galactic Dawn* a few weeks ago. If they were already here manipulating trilobites, why bother trying to infiltrate a colony ship full of trained soldiers?

Maybe all of that was just for show, I thought, providing the answer to my own question. Had all of that been misdirection? Was that squad sent to be captured, all so we could rest easy in our overconfidence? Was I being played for a fool?

I felt my shoulders tense at the thought. There was so much I didn't know, and I couldn't stand being in the dark.

"Captain?" asked Dressler, breaking through my thoughts.

I blinked at the sound of her voice. "Sorry," I said, clearing my throat. "I was just weighing our options."

"Did you come to a decision?" she asked.

"We're going," I said quickly but firmly. "If we want to survive on this planet for the long haul, we need to understand what the hell is happening. It means taking a risk, but none of us are strangers to that. Right, Freddie?"

He nodded. "Right."

"What about the new colonists?" asked Abigail. "Someone needs to stay behind to help make the transition."

I hesitated to answer. I'd forgotten about the new arrivals. They would need new rooms, food, and other supplies before things were settled, and we couldn't let them wander around the colony on their own. Who knew what they might do? We also couldn't keep them on the *Dawn* for much longer. It had already been a month. They might riot if we kept them cooped up, especially with the Earth staring at them through their windows. "Any volunteers?" I asked.

"I'll go where you need me," said Bolin.

I shook my head at Bolin. "I need you to pilot one of our ships. Anyone else?"

"I can stay behind," said Karin. "I'm certain the rest of the *Galactic Dawn*'s crew would be eager to join me too."

It was a tough decision. I could always use Karin's expertise, given what she knew about ancient Earth technology. She spoke the language, understood how to use their systems, but so could Dressler, and we didn't need both of them.

"Don't forget about Dr. Hitchens," interjected Freddie. "I'm sure he'll volunteer to help."

"Where is he anyway?" asked Abigail. "I'm surprised he's not here."

"He's busy helping the cleaning crew organize the new classroom," said Octavia.

"How do you already know about that?" I asked.

"He met me when I landed," she said. "He always does."

"Isn't that sweet?" asked Lucia, finally cutting in with a snide remark. "Enough prattling. Let's get on with this. I have things to do."

"Looks like you'll have to decide, Captain," said Alphonse. "Which of us stays behind while the rest plunge headfirst into the belly of the world?"

I STOOD next to my strike ship, pistol on my hip and a satchel on my shoulder. Several other vessels were currently landing on the east side of Verdun, each one carrying a few dozen new colonists.

I had asked Karin, Hitchens, and a handful of other people to manage and corral the new colonists while the rest of us were away. We had to get them new accommodations, jobs, food, and eventually brief them on exactly what it was we were trying to do here. I preferred to do the last bit myself, but given the task ahead of us, I decided to wait until we returned to the colony. For now, my team would accommodate our new friends as much as possible. We'd worry about explaining their future to them at a later date.

The good news was that we would finally have more help in and around the colony. That meant more labor for the crops, cleaning out the remaining buildings, and a laundry list of other tasks that we simply didn't have the time to do with our small workforce. It was hard work building a civilization, but I was certain we could do it once we had the numbers behind us. With enough people behind a cause, anything is achievable.

The sight of those ships landing was a nice reminder that we were making progress.

"Ready to go?" asked Abigail, poking her head out from inside the ship. "Or would you prefer to stand there all day gawking?"

I gave her a look that suggested she had better watch the sarcasm, but it only made her snicker.

Freddie was approaching the landing pad as we spoke, but the other two crew members from *Titan* were already onboard. I had decided it might be a good idea to bring a few folks with some expertise on the mission, particularly when it came to ancient Earth tech. Each of them had been hand-picked by Dressler herself. She was currently riding in one of the other strike ships, but six members of her team made up roughly a quarter of our squadron.

I also made an effort to select a handful of well-trained soldiers from among Lucia's team. After all, there was no telling what we'd find at the bottom of that pit. For all I knew, we were walking into a den of trilobites, each one deadly enough to kill a grown man. At the same time, there was a small chance we could stumble upon a cache of ancient technology and we might need engineers proficient enough to figure out what it all meant. The fact of the matter was that we simply didn't know.

My time as a Renegade had taught me plenty, but the most important thing had always been to prepare for every possible outcome. That was especially true right now as we readied ourselves for the unknown.

"Captain!" called Freddie, waving at me as he neared.

"It's about time," I said, smacking his back. "Glad you decided to join us."

He smiled. "Do you think Karin and Dr. Hitchens can handle the new arrivals?"

"I'd wager so. They've got plenty of help, including the rest of your ship's crew."

"Crew?" he asked.

"From the *Galactic Dawn*," answered Abigail, poking out from inside the ship again. "I had a handful join the colonists. Jace and I agree that a few familiar faces might help with the transition."

Freddie paused. "Can I ask which crew members?"

"Does it matter?" asked Abigail. "They're all competent enough for the task."

I snickered. "Don't worry, Freddie. Petra's not on the list."

He seemed to relax, drooping his shoulders. "I-I see."

"Did someone say my name?" asked Petra from inside the ship.

"Yeah," I continued, still looking at Freddie with a composed look on my face. "She's coming with us."

He stiffened, his eyes widening. "W-what?!"

Abigail feigned surprise. "Did you forget to tell him? That was very irresponsible of you, Jace." She shook her head. "Poor Frederick."

"Sorry about that, pal. Looks like you're just gonna

have to deal with this little problem of yours," I said, finally stepping into the ship. "Good luck."

"Is that Frederick?" asked Petra.

Freddie visibly gulped, his skin turning chalk white in the process. I'd never seen the boy so intimidated. "Y-yeah, I'm here, Petra," he called, climbing inside.

"There you are!" she exclaimed, reaching out her hand from beneath her seat harness. "Didn't you see me earlier chasing after you? I was trying to tell you that—"

"Save the talk for later, you two," I barked, silencing them. "We've got a job to do right now."

I strapped into the pilot's seat, then tossed a mobile emitter on the dash. Sigmond appeared in a quick flash, his body approximately fifteen centimeters in height. He looked at me with his golden eyes and smiled. "I see we are ready to go. Very good, sir."

"Siggy, I want you watching those scans at all times," I told him. "The second you see anything dangerous, let me know."

"Understood, sir," he agreed. "Shall I inform the others that you are ready to depart?"

I tapped the comm in my ear. "I think I can handle that much," I said. "Boys and girls, this is Hughes. I want all ships in the sky in five minutes. No stragglers."

"We'll be right beside you," said Octavia, who was piloting one of the other ships.

"Same for us," said Alphonse.

"And us," added Bolin.

Altogether, we had four ships, each one piloted by a pilot I knew could handle the worst of it. Bolin, Alphonse, and Octavia were all at the top of their class.

Second only to me, of course.

The engines primed, and we lifted off the landing platform and into the free air, making for a smooth transition. I told the ship to move towards the eastern horizon, taking us away from Verdun, high above the clouds.

The other ships were right behind me, each of them equal distance apart. It would take us an hour to reach the chasm, bringing us across two continents and an ocean in the process.

6

We reached the chasm a few minutes earlier than expected. The sun was at its highest point and the wind remained calm with no sign of any hard weather.

Trilobites scurried along the dirt near the edge of the pit, exactly as Octavia had described them. I had never seen so many in one place before. I wagered none of us had before today. They crept and crawled from inside the hole, and I could only imagine how many remained unseen, deep inside the darkened earth.

The moment we were close enough for the scanners to register, a small holo appeared on the dash, floating beside Sigmond. It was a direct line-of-sight layout of the pit, the best we could get for right now, but one that would slowly grow and build the more we explored.

I touched the comm on my ear and signaled the other

ships. "Follow my lead but put some distance between yourselves. Octavia, you hold the rear. Everyone else, stay between us, keep your wits, and try not to crash on your way down."

"Understood," said Alphonse.

The others were quick to agree, no objections among them. Once we'd formed our ship order, I edged my way closer to the chasm, enough so we were only about twelve meters from the ground.

The trilobites moved without interruption, giving no acknowledgement to our presence. Perhaps they knew, somehow, that we were no threat to their work, or maybe they simply didn't care. Hard to say, since those creatures were still a mystery to us, but they were a question for another time.

For now, only the pit mattered.

We began our descent once everyone was in position, edging cautiously into the dark. I kept us moving at the same pace the scanners revealed the space ahead. The last thing I wanted was to go careening into a wall or an obscured ledge.

"How far do you think it goes?" asked Freddie, staring out his window.

"It can't be more than thirty kilometers," said Petra

"You think so?" asked her associate, whose name I thought was Verne, though I hadn't taken the time to find out.

"There's no way this goes further than that," she insisted.

"You sound pretty sure of yourself," said Abigail from the front passenger's seat. She didn't bother turning around.

"That's because the records show thirty kilometers is about the average thickness of the planet's crust," explained Petra. "If this hole is any deeper than that, I can't imagine we'll be able to follow it to completion."

"She raises a good point," I said.

"Are you a geologist now?" asked Abigail.

I sidestepped the question by going straight to Sigmond. "What do you think?" I asked, looking at the little Cognitive on the dashboard.

He stroked his chin thoughtfully, although I couldn't imagine why. "Petra raises an interesting thought."

"See?" asked Petra.

Verne shrugged.

"However," continued Sigmond, "given the advances in technology made since Athena's departure from Earth, the Eternals may have found a way to burrow beyond the planet's crust. For that matter, the geology could have changed to accommodate the terraforming process, making for a thicker layer than the previous iteration. I'm afraid there are simply too many unknowns."

Verne looked at Petra. "You were saying?"

"Never mind," she relented.

"Do not be discouraged," said Sigmond, a bit of cheer

in his voice. "Our scans are revealing more data by the moment."

"Exactly," said Abigail. "Wait a bit and you just may find yourselves with more answers than questions."

"Or the opposite," I countered. "Truth is, we don't much know, one way or the other."

Abigail and Sigmond both nodded. "Indeed," said the Cognitive.

As we continued our descent, the holo filled, and with every centimeter of light came more definition to the walls. We did this for a while—nearly three hours—dropping through the endless, never-changing pit. It was devoid of anything, except for the trilobites, each one scuttling along the stone walls like insects. There were hundreds of them, I guessed, creeping between the cracks, coming and going to gods-knew-where.

It was like burrowing inside an anthill, only the ants were as big as a small child.

"Jace," said Abigail, once some time had passed. "Do you think we made a mistake coming down here together and leaving Verdun to the others?"

I could hear Freddie and the others talking behind us, immersed in a discussion about the trilobites. Petra was explaining a theory of hers, although I couldn't hear much of it from the front seat. I glanced over at Abigail, trying to ignore the mumbling behind us, and chose to focus my attention on her. "You don't think Hitchens and Karin can handle things?"

"I'm certain they can," she answered. "But this is the first group we've brought home. I didn't think much about it at the time, but in hindsight—"

"You think we made a mistake," I finished.

She nodded. "At a time like this, when things are still so fragile?" she asked, pausing. "Maybe."

I checked the time. "It's just after midday, which means they should be in their new rooms. We've got time left in the day to make it back and deal with any major problems that come up. Once we're at the bottom, we'll—"

The holo flashed red, pulling our attention to Alphonse's ship as it brushed against the pit wall. I watched the vessel ignite its stabilization thrusters, pushing away from the rockface and reorienting itself in the middle of the chasm.

A second later, something hit the top of our ship, shaking our hull with a loud thud. We held our seats, tension on all our faces, but the ship settled quickly with no sign of damage. I guessed it was a rock, then signaled Alphonse, asking what the hell had just happened.

"I'm not entirely certain," he said quickly, an uncharacteristic sense of confusion in his voice. "We were flying normally and then I lost control."

"Siggy, run a system diagnostic," I ordered. "Bring all ships to a stop."

"Already underway, sir," said the Cognitive. The holo magnified Alphonse's ship so it took up most of the dash. There was a short pause while the data processed and the check concluded. "It appears one of the ship's sensors is misaligned. I'm correcting it now."

"How the hell did that happen?" I asked.

"Unknown, sir. As advanced as these vessels are, they are not beyond the occasional problem, like any working machine." Sigmond pointed to the holo, which showed the ship's sensors in red. "Rebooting system now."

The light changed from red to green, suggesting things were back to normal. "How we looking?" I asked.

"All systems appear to be operational," said Sigmond. "Mr. Malloy, you are free to resume control."

"Thank you, Sigmond," said Alphonse. "I apologize for our negligence, Captain."

"Not your fault," I assured him.

Abigail touched the side of my chair. "This might be a good time to leave," she said. "We can come back later once the maintenance crew has a chance to—"

"What was that?" asked Petra, cutting her off. She sounded rattled, so I turned around to see what was wrong. She was looking around the compartment, like she was searching for something. "Did you hear that?"

"Hear what?" I asked.

She held up a finger to quiet everyone then pointed to the upper hull. "Listen."

We did as she suggested, saying nothing, and straining to hear whatever she was talking about. I was about to tell her it was all in her head, when it happened again—a sudden, light tapping sound, steadily beating against the outside of the ship. It was the same spot where the rock had fallen moments ago.

"What is that?" asked Abigail.

"Might be pieces of the walls," suggested Verne. "You know, from where the other ship hit."

"Or rain," said Freddie.

I turned back to Sigmond. "Do sensors show anything?"

"Weather is clear, and I detect no falling objects, sir," said Sigmond.

"That doesn't make sense," said Abigail, looking at me. "A sound like that doesn't just materialize out of nothing. It has to have a source."

I nodded then tapped my ear. "Octavia, this is Hughes. I need a favor."

"I hear you, Captain," she responded.

"What are you doing?" asked Abigail.

"If we can't use sensors, we'll have to check it out the old-fashioned way," I said. "Octavia, fly down closer to my position. Examine our hull and send the feed directly to me. There's something on top of us and I'd like to know what it is."

"Isn't Alphonse's ship closer?" asked Freddie.

"His ship might still be having problems," I countered. "Best to play it safe."

"We're on the move now, Captain," said Octavia. "Hold, please."

When the comm went quiet, so did the rest of the ship.

We sat in silence, waiting for Octavia to get into position, and the sound of the tapping from outside the hull grew louder. It filled the cabin with a steady, constant beating.

All our eyes were fixed on the ship's ceiling, at the spot where the sound seemed to be the loudest, and the vibrations the strongest.

"Captain?" called Octavia, her voice causing me to blink. I pivoted back in my seat to the holo.

"Go ahead," I said.

The video feed popped up on the dash, showing the inside of the pit. Octavia's ship had its outer light fixed to the top of ours. From there, I could see most of our hull, but only barely. The light seemed to reflect off of us so much that it made it difficult to see. I was about to ask her to dim it, when the light flickered.

And then it moved.

"What the—"

A loud cracking sound cut me off before I could get the final word out. Something dropped and slammed into the middle of our cabin floor, right between my chair and Petra's.

I nearly leapt out of my seat as everyone frantically tried to move away.

There was a trilobite sitting inside the ship, its mandibles clicking and clapping, almost like an insect. The spot above us had somehow melted away, although there was no smoke or steam.

Abigail tried to hastily unbuckle her harness, simultaneously reaching for her rifle.

The trilobite scuttled along the floor, first to Freddie, who cringed at the sight of it. "Get it away!" he screamed.

"Stay calm!" ordered Abigail.

Petra unbuckled her harness and, just as the trilobite was about to touch Freddie, kicked it.

The trilobite paused briefly, almost like it was readjusting, and then made a hard dash towards Petra. It scurried up the side of her seat.

She yelped and pulled away, but the trilobite caught her arm and clamped it down against the chair. Immediately, it let out a sound that could only be described as sizzling.

Petra screamed as the trilobite liquified her entire arm, melting flesh and bone at the same time.

All of this happened in seconds.

I yanked my pistol from the spot beneath my chair, pulled around, and aimed at the trilobite.

Petra collapsed to the side, her entire arm gone. Meanwhile, the trilobite was busy consuming its juices, using its mandibles to suck up the liquid.

I fired into its backside, but the shock of the bullet only caused it to flinch. When it didn't respond, I shot again, piercing its shell for the second time.

Abigail, who'd finally managed to get her vest free and her gun ready, joined me in the assault. The trilobite took it all, so much more interested in consuming the arm than about its own well-being.

We continued until it finally let go of its grip on the seat and collapsed on the floor, motionless as it bled organic liquid from its chest—an orange goo that stank like shit and copper.

Freddie rushed to Petra, who had already passed out. Her forehead was covered in sweat, but she was breathing. Freddie gave me a quick nod to confirm this, and I swiveled back around in my seat, touching the control pad and ordering my ship to return home.

"Captain, what's going on over there?" asked Alphonse. "I'm detecting gunfire and—"

"Get your ships out of here," I ordered, breaking in. "Siggy, call ahead and tell them to prep the med pod."

"Was someone hurt?" asked Octavia.

"Yeah, one of the trilobites broke in," I answered, flying past the other ships. "Get your asses clear of this pit and, whatever you do, stay away from the godsdamn walls."

7

THE MED POD was inside one of the rooms near my office. Like so many other facilities we'd thrown together in the last few months, this was never meant to be permanent. In fact, the med pods should have been moved to a larger space weeks ago, but since our only medical issues involved a twisted ankle and a mild case of dehydration, we'd just never gotten around to it.

In other words, this shit was on me, and I damn well knew it.

We rushed Petra into the room while Dressler powered on the machine. "It may take a few moments for the pod's system to boot," explained the doctor.

"How long?" asked Octavia.

"Five minutes," said Dressler.

"Why wasn't it already set up?!" asked Freddie, filled with so much fear, I thought he might pass out.

"It requires power, and we're running on generators at the moment," explained Dressler. "Now, if you have a spare Tritium core sitting around somewhere that I don't know about—"

"Put her inside the pod," I interrupted, looking at Freddie. "Okay?"

"O-okay," he muttered. "Inside."

Dressler raised the lid and pulled it to the side, allowing us to gently set an unconscious Petra inside the device. Once she was in, the doctor closed the seal and finally proceeded to activate the startup sequence.

Athena manifested beside the doctor, appearing in a quick flash of blue light. Her eyes fell on the girl in the pod, but she remained as composed as ever. "Assessing damage," said the Cognitive. "I can take it from here, Doctor. Thank you."

Dressler nodded and motioned for everyone to move away from the pod. "Give her some space, please."

Freddie stepped back, but his eyes stayed on the glass. "Do you think—" He paused, fidgeting his hands. "—it can fix her? Can it regrow her—" He swallowed. "—her arm?"

"I don't know," I said honestly.

"It fixed Octavia's legs," he went on. "That's a good sign, right?"

I didn't answer this time. I only stood there, watching as Athena did her work. The hard-light constructs inside the pod materialized, each one giving off a faint glow. They moved carefully around Petra's shoulder, quickly sealing the exposed flesh, cooling it, and then providing the new layer of skin.

"The process will require some time," said Athena, looking directly at Freddie. "Her body will need to rest for several hours, but you may stay if you wish."

Freddie stepped closer to the pod, placing a hand on the glass as the light illuminated his face. It was clear he wouldn't be leaving anytime soon.

Dressler turned away from the pod and walked up beside me, nudging my arm with her own. "A word," she whispered before leaving for the outer hall.

Abigail was already there, watching from a distance. She and I followed Dressler to my office, a few rooms down the hall, and I made sure to close the door behind us.

"I hate to be like this, but we need to talk about that machine," said Dressler, keeping her voice down.

"The pod?" I asked.

"I think she means the trilobite," answered Abigail.

"Oh, *that*," I said. "What about it?"

"It needs to be dissected and analyzed so that we may find a solution to—"

"Is this really the best time for that?" asked Abigail.

Dressler paused, probably more out of courtesy than anything. "There's nothing we can do about Petra right now," she continued after a moment. "She's in a sophisticated medical pod, with one of the most advanced life-forms in the galaxy looking after her. I'm not sure the three of us will make much of a difference in that room."

"Frederick might disagree," said Abigail.

"Perhaps so," conceded the doctor. "But he is not in the right state of mind to see things objectively, and I would caution the two of you to take a step back."

"You don't think we're thinking clearly?" I asked.

"Your friend is in distress. It is natural to feel a desire to help him," she explained.

"And you don't feel that?" asked Abigail.

"On the contrary," answered Dressler. "I feel it very much. The difference is that I choose to take a more practical approach to how I react. What happened to Petra is done and cannot be reversed, but we may yet find a way to see that nothing like this ever happens again."

"What did you have in mind?" I asked, sitting on the edge of my desk and crossing my arms.

"As I said, dissection of the machine, for a start," she said.

"And after that?" I asked.

"Simply put, Captain, if we can understand what makes it tick, we may yet find a way to deactivate it. At the very least, it will teach us something we don't already know, and that is always a good thing."

I couldn't argue with that. The woman might be cold, but she certainly knew how to make her case. "I had Verne take the trilobite to a separate area to watch until we were done here," I explained.

"On this floor?" she asked.

"Different building," I said. "The one we're in the middle of clearing out."

Abigail cocked her brow. "Where the new classroom is?"

"The very same," I said matter-of-factly.

"Jace, don't tell me you had them drop that death machine off in the classroom itself," said Abby.

"Fine, I won't tell you that," I said with a shrug.

She scowled at me, but I ignored it. "Doc, if you want that thing dissected, you'd best get on it soon. I want that thing out of this city within the next twelve hours."

"That might not be enough time," she cautioned.

"I don't care," I replied. "If the new arrivals see or hear about it, if they find out we've got a trilobite—even a dead one—they'll lose their collective shit."

Dressler seemed to understand my point, so she didn't argue, but she made no effort to hide her annoyance. "I'll need to be fast, then. If you wouldn't mind, Captain, I'd like to borrow Sigmond."

As soon as she said his name, Sigmond appeared beside us, causing both women to flinch. "Gods," Abigail blurted out.

"I'm morc than happy to assist you, Doctor," said Sigmond.

Dressler relaxed and nodded. "I take it I won't need to explain everything again, Sigmond?"

"You assume correctly," he answered.

"Good," she said, then looked at me. "Would you be so kind as to lend me that mobile emitter, Captain?"

I reached in my pocket and tossed it to her. So far, my office and most of this floor were the only areas in the city with active emitters already installed, which meant I had to carry that spiffy piece of tech around with me everywhere I went. I didn't much like the idea of lending it out, but special circumstances and all that. "Don't break it," I said plainly.

She scoffed. "You forget who I am, Captain."

I THOUGHT about going with Dressler to dissect the trilobite, and very nearly did, until Abigail talked me into staying.

"Freddie needs us here," she said once Dressler had taken the mobile emitter and left the office. "That woman knows what she's doing better than either of us."

I grunted my agreement, but the truth was I had little interest in sitting in that room and watching my friend suffer beside that pod. None of it would do anyone any good. Dressler, for all her practicality, had been right about that.

Still, Freddie was my friend and I was willing to stand there with him if it made the moment easier for him to bear, although I suspected it wouldn't.

Hours passed, yet the three of us remained. Freddie

kept beside the pod, always watching from the other side of the glass, while Abigail and I stayed against the wall, near the door. A light would blink occasionally, stirring Freddie's attention and giving him a palpable sense of dread. Had something gone wrong? Was the machine having problems?

No, nothing at all, and we all knew as much, yet it plagued Freddie all the same.

Eventually, the screen beside the pod changed, drawing our attention, and Athena appeared beside us. "I apologize for the delay, everyone," she said, walking to the end of the pod. "The graph has set. Would you like me to wake her?"

"What about the rest of her arm?" asked Freddie, confusion all over his face. "That can't be the end of it. Does she need to come back later?"

"No, not later," said Athena, frowning at the man before her. "There are limits to the regeneration pods. They can repair nerves and tissue, but they cannot grow a limb."

Freddie's eyes widened briefly, and then he sank back into his chair. In that moment, I suddenly saw what it meant for him to be truly defeated. Through all our battles, all our trials and tribulations, I had never seen him in this way.

I had to say, I didn't like it. "There has to be something," I said, still watching him. "Athena, I know you can do more."

"Can't you regrow organs?" asked Abigail. "Karin said you had the ability."

"Organs, yes," said the Cognitive. "But I'm afraid—"

"Whole limbs are different," muttered Freddie.

Athena looked at him then slowly nodded. "Yes."

I got to my feet and walked to Freddie's side, placing a hand on his shoulder. "Go ahead and wake her, then."

"As you wish," said Athena.

Abigail joined us at the pod. "When she opens her eyes, she'll react based on how we look. If we seem distressed, she'll panic, so we have to look collected and calm."

I squeezed Freddie's shoulder. "He gets it," I said. "Don't you, Fred?"

He nodded, sitting up in his seat and pretending to smile. It wasn't much—no teeth or the goofy grin I was so used to—but it was enough for what he needed it to be. Enough to make it through the worst hour of that poor woman's life.

8

Petra was better about the arm than I'd expected. She didn't cry or scream when she saw it, but there was a clear sense of loss in her eyes. An empty look where rage and fear should be, but I recognized it for it was.

Shock.

The tears would come later, maybe tonight or tomorrow. Maybe in a week. But they would come, and it would rip her apart.

Freddie would be there for all of it, not because he had to be, but because he wanted to, with every piece of himself. I knew it the second he leapt across the ship.

Whatever reservations Freddie had about meeting that woman's parents, it was clear how he felt about her. He just didn't understand how deeply she'd infected him with it.

But I knew.

"Dressler says she thinks she can have something by tomorrow," said Abigail, her cheek buried in my chest as we lay together in my bed. "I told her it will have to wait until after we address the new arrivals."

"Smart," I said, staring into the darkness of the room. It was after midnight and I had to be up in five hours. My eyes burned from exhaustion, but my mind couldn't let the day go.

Abigail turned her head to look at me, and I caught a flicker of light in her eye. "Where are you right now?" she asked. "You feel so far away."

"I was just asking myself the same thing," I said.

"Were you?" she asked.

I gave her a soft grunt. "We've come all the way to Earth, and still, it's all a mystery. Dead soil, cities in the sky, and trilobites. I don't know what to make of any of it."

"Does that mean you regret coming here?"

I considered that question for a second, but then dismissed it. "No. It's not that. I just need to know what I'm up against."

"Does that bother you?" she asked. "Not knowing the variables?"

"I've always had a plan," I told her. "And when that plan failed, I had another ready to take its place. I can't do that here. There's too much we just don't know."

"But we can find out," she responded. "Dressler is working on that trilobite right now. We might wake in the morning to hear she's discovered something."

"Maybe," I conceded. "Whatever happens, we'll still need to go back inside that pit, and when we do, I don't know if I'll be able to protect everyone."

She smiled. "You know," she said, nudging herself closer to my neck. "For a brigand and an outlaw, you care an awful lot about your friends."

"Don't start with that again," I said, wrapping my arm around her shoulder. "I'll boot your ass out of bed."

She smacked my chest. "Try it and see what happens."

BENEATH A BLANKET OF STORM CLOUDS, I struggled to breathe.

Brigham's hand gripped my throat, squeezing with such intensity that the prospect of dying seemed like an absolute certainty.

An inevitability.

"You lose, Hughes!" said the old, ragged man as blood seeped from the wound in his cheek. "Let yourself die with some dignity."

His eyes were savage, like a deranged animal's. There was fire in them, burning at the prospect of my death, and it fueled him. This man, this monster, who'd chased me across a galaxy—he'd never give up until everything I loved was reduced to ash.

I pushed against him with all the force I had in me. "Sorry, Marcus," I wheezed, reaching inside his helmet for a piece of his shattered visor, slicing my own fingers in the process. "Ain't never had much in the way of dignity."

I pulled my hand up then slammed it down in the soft spot between his neck and chest piece, burying the shard and twisting.

He screamed with such intensity that it hurt my ears, the agony of pain like a demon's shriek, but I knew I had him. I knew I had won.

But then he stopped his wailing and instead went still and cold, closing his mouth and looking down at me again with the most vacant expression I'd ever seen on him.

The shard in his neck was still there, blood oozing out of him, sliding down his skin and through his clothes before pooling in his shirt. His eyes widened, and his lips twisted into a thin smile, showing blackened, razor-sharp teeth. "They're coming for you, Jace."

I stiffened at the sound of my name.

"The whole fucking galaxy is coming for you and that girl."

"Quiet!" I barked.

"Everything you've built is going to burn because of what you've done," he said in a voice I no longer recognized. It was deeper, more vile and toxic, almost otherworldly. "All because of you, Jacey!"

Brigham's eyes morphed and twisted, his face changing into a disfigured blob of flesh, the shard still in his neck, bobbing and moving as the meat continued to shift and bend.

"Jacey," he said, but not from a mouth. There was no more mouth, eyes, or nose. "Jacey, Jacey, Jacey."

My chest heaved as my heart began to pound like a drum in my chest, ready to explode. I reached up and took the shard, yanking it free of the meat. Blood sprayed out like a hose, filling the air with mist. "Shut the fuck up!" I raged, jamming the glass inside his throat, up beneath his jaw and into his brain.

Brigham let out a scream so loud, it tore the sky asunder, replacing gray with red. I clutched my ears with both hands and screamed.

I was going to die. Everyone was going to die.

By the gods, what have I done?

I WOKE IN A COLD SWEAT, heart racing and breathing heavily.

Abigail stirred the second I sat up, but she didn't wake right away.

I sat there for a long moment, trying to calm down. It took me a second to orient myself, to remember where I was and what I was doing here. I had to remind myself that the fight with Brigham that had been months ago, far away from this planet. He was dead and buried now, no threat to anyone.

And yet, the old man's words still haunted me like needles tapping the back of my brain. He'd warned me that the Union would never stop chasing me, told me I'd always be on the run, and I believed it. They'd been crippled, sure, but never killed. Those people wanted Lex, the Earth, and all the potential they represented. I had to stay ahead of them, keep my eyes open for any signs of movement, searching for any hint of a threat or sabotage.

When they attacked—and I was sure they would—the rest of us would have to be ready.

After a quick shower, I guzzled down two cups of coffee to make up for the lack of rest, and then rushed out to my office. Sigmond was already standing there when I walked in, waiting to greet me with his usual, pleasant smile.

"Good morning, sir," said the Cognitive. "Are you prepared for today's schedule?"

"Not even a little," I commented, picking up the pad on my desk. Twenty minutes to go before I was set to meet the new colonists, which only gave me a short while to grab some food from my cabinet.

I snatched a small chocolate muffin I'd stolen from *Titan*'s storage locker and ripped into it with a quick bite. It was gone in less than a minute, but I didn't mind. That might be the only food I'd have all morning.

Entering the hallway, I spotted a cracked door—the one for the temporary medical room in which we'd placed the pod. As I approached, the pod slowly came into view, along with the nearby seat and the figure sitting in it.

Freddie was fast asleep beside Petra, his arms hanging

on the side of the open pod, still wearing the same clothes as yesterday.

I thought about waking him but decided against it. For him to still be here, he must have been awake for half the night.

Standing next to the door, I let out a long sigh then turned away. As I did, I heard something stir from inside the room. "Captain?" whispered a voice. "Is that you?"

Looking back, I saw Petra, her eyes half open from inside the pod. "Sorry," I muttered, uncertain of whether I should stay or leave. "I was just checking on the two of you."

"Frederick told me what happened," she whispered, glancing at him as he slept.

So this wasn't the first time she'd awoken. That saved me from having to explain the situation to her. "How are you feeling?"

"There's not much pain," she said like it surprised her.

"That's not what I meant," I said.

She lowered her eyes. "I keep trying to move it, but there's nothing there. It's jarring. I suppose I'll get used to it."

"They call that phantom limb," I explained. "It's not uncommon. The good news is that there are options. Dressler thinks we can get you an artificial arm in under a week. You'll just have to go through some rehab work."

She nodded. "Athena mentioned something about it."

"You don't seem very happy about that," I observed.

"With all due respect, sir," she began, "I can't imagine anything artificial ever living up to the real thing. Can you?"

"I don't suppose I can, Petra."

She smiled, although there was a sadness to it, like the kind you give at a funeral to the widow of a friend. She touched Freddie's head, gently rubbing his hair. "He stayed with me through the night, you know."

I nodded.

"Most women would have seen the way he ran when he left the ship and assumed the worst, but I knew better."

"The way he ran?" I asked, trying to play ignorant. "What do you mean?"

"I'm no fool, sir. I knew he felt intimidated by the prospect of meeting my family, but that doesn't mean his feelings were any less sincere." Her eyes warmed as she said the words, glancing again at Freddie. "He's been here the whole time, trying to act brave for me, but I know he's terrified. I can see it."

"He does it because he loves you," I said.

She nodded. "I know."

I stared at the two of them as she continued to stroke his hair, neither of us saying anything. After a little while, I leaned off the wall. "Petra," I said, calling her attention a final time. I waited until we locked eyes before I continued. "We'll figure this out. I'm promise you that."

With that, I left her to rest again, heading down the hall towards the exit. My day was only just getting started.

When I arrived outside, Hitchens was standing on the nearby stairs, waving the new arrivals to form up. They were sluggish, having just rolled out of bed. I expected a few to stay in their quarters, but that was fine. Whatever I said now would be circulated in the dorms over the next few days, one way or another.

"Thank you all for coming," said Hitchens, raising his arms to the settling crowd. "Today, we'll be dividing into groups and going over potential work assignments. If you have any experience in a particular field, regardless of what it might be, please let one of us know. We'll try to match you with a job that best suits your abilities. That should take up most of the morning, so once we're through, we'll break for lunch. After that, we'll break into our groups and you'll learn about your first major project."

The crowd stirred, inaudible chatter filling the square. Whispers, mostly, but a few choice words made their way to my ears.

"Is that the Renegade?" someone asked.

"There! I saw him on the ship!" said another.

Hitchens glanced at me, like he was giving me the floor.

I sighed but went along with it and stepped forward to the edge of the top step, right beside the archeologist. "Good morning," I said, raising my voice. The second I did, the chatter ceased. It was a surreal feeling, being able to control the attention of a mob. I wasn't sure I liked it. "I was supposed to be up here in front of you all sometime yesterday, but—" I paused, clearing my throat. "Well, let's just say the day got away from me."

"We heard someone got hurt," said a man in the front. "Is that true?"

The question threw me, although I knew it shouldn't have. Of course they already knew about the accident. In a colony this small, news traveled fast, so what was I really expecting?

"Yeah," I answered. "One of our crew took a bad hit. We went to investigate something on the surface and the situation took a turn. She's being treated right now in the med bay, but I won't lie to you. It isn't good."

The crowd stirred, whispering amongst themselves. I knew what they were feeling. Fear. Confusion. Regret. All of it compounded by the notion that maybe leaving their homes wasn't such a good idea after all.

"I'm not going to sit here and lie to you about how hard all of this is going to be," I shouted, instantly quieting them. When they settled, I paused, letting the silence fester until I was certain it could no longer last. "I came here because I wanted the same thing as all of you—the freedom to live by my own choices, and enough weight to throw around in case anyone tried to come and take it from me."

"The Union!" someone shouted.

"Fuck them!" yelled another.

I raised my hand to quiet them. "You say you hate the

Union. Well, so do I. So does everyone else on this planet. But you can't be free of them without doing the hard labor, without sweat and blood to keep you safe. That's the cost of having what you want. It's the wall you build to keep them out." I pointed behind me, towards the end of the hall inside the building. "Sometimes that means losing a little before you can win, and gods know we've a need to win. But let me just say this, and then you can decide what you want to do: one way or another, this colony is going to become what I aim for it to be, even if I have to build the whole damn thing with my own godsdamn hands. You want to do the work with me and call this your new home, then I promise you, that's what it'll be. Verdun is a city for you, built by you, and protected by you. It ain't no one else's, and it sure as hell ain't the Union's. You remember that, and you ask yourself if something that rare is worth hurting for—if it's worth dying for. If not, then you let Hitchens here know and he'll have you back aboard the *Dawn*, back to the Deadlands." I looked at Hitchens and he nodded. "As for the rest of you," I continued, "well, it's about time we got to work."

9

I STARED at the pad Hitchens had just handed to me. The screen listed each and every newly documented colonist, breaking them down into potential job categories. "Are these already assigned?" I asked.

Hitchens shook his head. "Not until we approve it."

"Sixteen for farming, twenty-two for services, eleven for engineering, and—" I paused. "—thirty-two for combat?"

"Those are based on previous work experience."

"Are you saying a third of these people have combat experience?" I asked.

Hitchens shifted his weight. "Well, some are former soldiers, but many others happen to have been, oh, shall we call them, *unlawful* citizens."

"Criminals?" I asked, glancing at the pad again, then

sighed. "Can't say I'm surprised. We *did* pick them up in the Deadlands."

"Yes, I suppose it does come with the territory," admitted Hitchens.

"What's this second line beneath the first job listing?" I asked.

"That would be the preferred occupation listing," said Hitchens. "I thought it might be a good idea to see what the individual wanted, rather than rely solely on their work experience."

Sure enough, beneath several of the colonists with combat experience, they'd listed something else, such as farming or services. There were even things we didn't offer, such as pilot, teacher, and cook. "Some of these aren't half bad," I conceded, scanning the new entries.

"I thought the same, although we aren't in need of them at the moment," said Hitchens.

"Well, we could use the extra soldiers, even if they are a little threatening," I said.

"Threatening?" asked Octavia, closing the door as she entered. She walked over to Hitchens and smiled at him.

"What I mean is, why not start them off elsewhere and see if they're trustworthy?" I asked.

"You're saying you'd rather get to know them first?" Octavia asked.

I thought back to the incident on the *Galactic Dawn* involving the drug addict and the way he threatened a family. That had only been with a knife. I couldn't imagine the outcome if he'd found a gun. "Since most of these people are strangers, I think it might be best."

"Speaking of which," said Octavia, "are we certain we want new soldiers at all?"

"You don't think we do?" I asked.

"We have an entire fleet of drones protecting us," she explained. "There's also Lucia's team, each of whom is capable enough to handle any policing that needs done."

"You saw what that trilobite did to Petra. She lost her arm in only a few seconds. Now imagine what might happen if those machines attack us. Hell, what if there's something else on this planet that aims to do us harm? It seems to me that having some capable fighters on our side might not be such a bad idea."

She nodded. "Had that incident not occurred, I might be inclined to disagree with you, but you raise a good point. We're in the unknown."

"But that doesn't mean we have to rush into anything," I added.

"No, it certainly doesn't," she agreed.

I handed the pad back to Hitchens. "Split the people with combat experience between the farmers and services. At that size, we'll be able to clear out a few more buildings by the end of the week, maybe even renovate them, and we can start a new garden on the other side of the square."

"Not bad," commented Octavia.

Hitchens placed his hand around her waist. "I believe the Captain is adapting well to his new role. Wouldn't you say?"

Before I could give them any shit for what they'd said, my comm clicked and pulled my attention away. "Captain, this is Dr. Dressler. I need you to come to the lab at once."

"What lab?" I asked. "You mean the classroom?"

"Yes, and right now it's a lab," she corrected. "I'll be waiting."

The comm clicked off. "Cheerful as ever," I muttered.

"Problems?" asked Octavia.

"Dressler says she's found something and she needs me to have a look," I said, walking to the door.

"Do tell us if she's found anything remarkable, would you?" asked Hitchens.

I motioned dismissively with my hand as I walked out the door. "You'll be the first."

Dressler stood in front of me with a pair of thick goggles that I'd never seen before as she examined the trilobite on the table. "I won't lie to you, Captain," she said. "The technology used to create this machine is more sophisticated than either Athena or I anticipated."

I said nothing, sensing there was more to it than that.

"However," she continued, flipping around to the trilobite. She picked up one of its severed legs and brought it up for me to see. “The dissection was not a complete failure. While we were unable to examine the operating system, its sensors were a different story.”

“How can you tap into the sensors without using the operating system?” I asked, staring into my own reflection from the goggles.

“The sensors are made up of physical parts. More hardware than software, really, but it gives us some insight into how they operate.”

“That’s good news,” I said.

“Quite so,” she agreed. “However, while the hardware may tell us how the sensors work, the software keeps us from getting access. In simple terms, that means we can’t control the trilobites or—”

“Shut them down,” I finished, letting out a long sigh.

“Correct,” she said, setting down the trilobite’s leg.

“So we’re still stuck,” I said, not bothering to hide my agitation.

“Maybe not,” she answered, looking at Sigmond, who was standing quietly by the wall. “Would you mind?”

“Not at all,” said Sigmond. He reached out his hand and another holo appeared above his fingertips. It was the trilobite, only smaller and in a state of constant motion, crawling along an invisible ground. “This model represents the machine’s standard rate of movement. Based on the sensory lens and its other hardware, we believe these machines are using a form of echolocation.”

“Echo *what*?” I asked.

"They're blind in the traditional sense," said Dressler. "They respond and react based on auditory stimuli. *Sound*, in other words."

The hologram of the trilobite suddenly emitted a pulse of gold light, which left Sigmond's hand and bounced off my chest, returning to it. The trilobite received the pulse, then moved towards me and raised its legs, like it was going to attack.

"Alright, I get it," I said, swiping my hand through the hologram, disrupting the light and momentarily scattering the image of the trilobite. "But why not have them use normal eyesight like any other drone?"

"I have a theory," said Dressler, walking to the holo on the counter. She typed a command, zooming out from the single trilobite so that it was standing on the ground, high above my head. Beneath it, there was nothing but dirt stretching all the way to the table. She typed another key and the trilobite started moving, burrowing into the ground. "We've seen a small portion of the machines wandering around on the surface, but as you may have noticed during our expedition through the chasm, there are thousands more beneath our feet. Without proper sunlight, the machines would need another form of vision to maneuver properly in the dark."

"Hence their echolocation," finished Sigmond.

"Why not just give them a light source?" I asked.

"Perhaps the Eternals found this system more energy

conservative," said Dressler. "Frankly, without sufficient information on their intentions, I couldn't say for certain."

I looked at Sigmond. "What good is any of this if we can't shut them *down*?"

"I believe she was getting to that, sir," explained the Cognitive.

Dressler waited for me to look at her again before she continued. "You must understand, Captain, knowing how these machines perceive the world around them is an *extraordinary* discovery."

"Oh?" I asked, crossing my arms. "And how's that?"

"You'll recall how the machine first noticed us," she said, jogging my memory.

"Alphonse's ship hit the rocks and knocked it down," I said.

"That is only partially accurate," she corrected. "Sensors show that the trilobite reacted to the ship, skittling from the rock to the wing on its own volition. It was at this point that the machine lost its footing and fell."

"Are you saying it saw Alphonse's ship, then tried to board it?" I asked.

She raised a finger. "Not saw," she corrected. "Heard."

"Right, right," I said. "Echolocation."

"Correct, Captain, but what I find most fascinating is this." She brought up the image of the trilobite as it had been on the chasm wall. There were several others around it, maybe eight of them, all remaining perfectly still. Then, as the wing of the ship touched the rock, the trilobite moved onto it, with two others following after. All of this was shown to me at twenty percent speed.

Once it was over, I asked her to run it again, just to make sure I had it.

As the holo replayed, I watched the trilobites, looking for whatever it was that Dressler had found. The first one grabbed hold of the wing, same as before, but the others—

"Stop there," I said, pointing to the trilobites near the edge of the holo. I took a step closer to them. "These aren't moving at all."

Dressler smiled. "Exactly."

"Why?" I asked, looking back at them. "Can't they sense the ship?"

"I've watched this several times, examining each and every trilobite. I've also observed the other feeds from both your ship as well as Octavia's. There are thousands of these machines inside the chasm, and yet—" She leaned away so that I could see the dead trilobite on the table. "—only this one and three others *reacted* to that ship."

"And they were all right next to where the wing hit," I added.

"Which means there is a limit to what they can hear," she explained.

"Approximately five meters, by my estimates," added Sigmond.

Dressler smiled. "A small window of visibility that I believe, given the right preparations, may yet be exploited."

"ALL OF THIS IS FINE, but we can't take a ship down in that chasm," said Abigail after Sigmond had explained the situation to her. I'd called her here, along with Alphonse and Octavia, hoping to get a handle on the situation and develop some kind of plan to deal with it.

"We're not," I replied, giving Sigmond a quick glance. "My boy here is sending one of his drones."

"A drone?" asked Alphonse. "Won't it lose its signal beyond a certain point?"

"That's correct," said Sigmond.

"Then what reason do you have for sending it?" asked the former spy.

Sigmond smiled. "The drone can be set to run a continuous scan in all directions as it descends. This will occur without user input, regardless of distance. Even if the drone loses contact, it will perform the scan and send its results every quarter second."

"We'll need to place a few signal repeaters, just in case that hole goes deeper than the drone can transmit," I said, tilting my head and giving him a look that suggested it wouldn't be easy. "But since the walls are lined with trilobites, that means we can't use them."

"If we can't touch the walls, then how do you plan on doing that?" asked Octavia.

"More drones," said Alphonse, smirking. "That's your plan, isn't it?"

"You know me too well, Al," I conceded. "Doc's already left for the *Dawn* to install the repeaters, one for each of the drones. She'll be done in—" I paused, looking at Sigmond. "How long was it?"

"Seven hours, sir," said the Cognitive.

"Seven hours," I repeated.

"I think I'm with you so far," said Abigail. "What's next?"

"Dunno," I admitted. "We'll see what's down there and decide if it's worth taking another risk. If it is, then at least we won't have to worry about flying in the dark."

Everyone agreed on the plan without much hesitation. After all, we weren't risking any lives by using a drone. Heading back inside, if we ever did, would be the point at which we'd have a more serious discussion, but I'd save that concern for when it mattered.

Alphonse began to leave when the meeting wrapped, but stopped at the door, doubling back like he'd forgotten something. "I meant to ask, but have we learned anything more about why the machines were trying to liquify Petra's arm?"

I blinked. "You're asking me?"

"I'm afraid without access to additional data, we still don't know," answered Sigmond.

Alphonse nodded, apparently satisfied with not knowing the answer. "Let me know if you figure it out, please."

"We have a working theory, if you would like to hear it," replied Sigmond.

Alphonse paused. "A theory?"

Sigmond smiled. "It is merely conjecture between Athena and me, but I think it holds promise."

"This is news to me," I said.

"Apologies, sir, but I didn't want to trouble you with anything until I knew for certain."

I walked over to where Abigail was sitting and joined her, taking the nearby seat. "Well, let's hear it, Siggy."

"As you know, the trilobites actively break down any foreign object that is not native to this planet. That also includes any materials from the elevated cities, such as Verdun."

We all nodded.

"Unless these machines are malfunctioning, I believe it stands to reason that such a protocol was intentionally designed by its creator, which implies it has a purpose."

"Which is what?" asked Abigail.

"Terraforming the planet," said Sigmond. "Or, more specifically, any objects that do not match a specific criteria. Consider the natural state of the world as it is right now—devoid of life and no sign of any former civilizations, save these elevated cities."

Alphonse's eyes widened, and he tapped his chin. "I think I see what you're getting at."

"You do?" I asked, cocking my head.

"This planet used to have plants and animals, didn't it?"

asked Alphonse. "Even if they all died from a rotting atmosphere, there should still be remnants of them. Bones, fossils, ruins, but so far, we've found nothing. Given what we know from Athena regarding the planet's history, it's as though the whole of it was wiped out."

"Or liquified," said Abigail.

"Precisely," said Sigmond.

"All of that material had to go somewhere," continued Alphonse. "Perhaps these trilobites are the cause of it."

Abigail scoffed. "Are you implying these machines terraformed everything on the planet?" she asked, pausing. "To a molecular level? All on their own?"

"I believe Sigmond and I are *both* implying it," said Alphonse.

Sigmond smiled. "Athena as well."

"But to do something like that on such a scale," said Octavia. "It would mean there are far more of those machines than what we've seen."

"Millions," added Sigmond. "That is, if our estimates hold true."

Octavia nodded. "Not only that, but if memory serves, when a trilobite collects its organic liquid, it returns underground."

"Which could mean they're storing it," said Abigail.

"Or using it," added Octavia. "But there's no way to know where any of this is taking place, is there?"

As soon as she asked the question, the answer seemed obvious to everyone in the room.

Sigmond looked towards the trilobite on the table. "It seems we have yet another reason to send our drones to the bottom of that chasm."

"Holy shit," I muttered.

Sigmond nodded. "Indeed."

10

THE IMPLICATION that the pit might hold a path to the trilobite nest sat with me for the rest of the evening. I couldn't tell you if it was the risk of inadvertently setting a swarm of terraforming death machines loose on the world or the fact that if we didn't do something, Verdun itself might be lost forever. Either way, something was about to happen here, and I wasn't sure I was ready to face it.

The following morning, I awoke at daybreak, too restless to go back to sleep. After only ten or so minutes, right when I was on the verge of hopping out of bed, I received a call. "Sir, I have Dr. Dressler for you," said Sigmond.

I turned on my side. "You just assume I'm awake, Siggy?"

"Your breathing and heart rate suggested you were, sir."

"Relax, pal. Put old MaryAnn through," I said.

"Right away, sir," he responded.

I heard a click, indicating I was connected. "What can I do for you, Doc?"

"Oh, splendid," she replied. "You're awake. I'm on my way to Verdun and wanted to make certain you were available when I arrived."

I twisted around in the bed, plopping my feet on the floor and cracking my neck. "I can be there in ten. What's the situation?"

"The drones have been augmented with repeaters, as we discussed, but I believe we'll need to reconfigure one of our ships as well."

"Why's that?" I asked.

"We may need to land once the drones have done their work."

"You think we'll need to leave the ship?" I asked.

"I don't know, truth be told, but fortune favors the prepared," she said. "Once the chasm has been sufficiently scanned, Sigmond will be able to navigate our strike ship with exact precision. I suggest transferring all controls to him and raising shields to full strength once we're inside."

I imagined how this might unfold, but without knowing what was actually inside the ground, it left me uneasy. Even with the drones and their scans, there was still potential for a surprise.

But we had little choice in the matter. Considering the growing number of terraforming bugs sitting idly below the city's scaffolding, something had to be done. If this mission provided the answers we needed, then it was worth the risk.

We hadn't spent this last month building Verdun for nothing.

"Assemble the crew and have them ready by mid-morning," I finally said.

"I will, but why not earlier? Do you have plans?" she asked.

"I'm going to check in on Freddie and Petra," I said.

"Ah," she said. "About that."

"What?"

"I was talking to Athena about the incident and I believe we may have something that can help."

"Something?" I repeated. "For Petra?"

"That's right. Why don't you meet me in the medical room? We can tell the girl together."

I DIDN'T GO STRAIGHT to see Petra. It would take Dressler several minutes longer before she made her way over to the building, which meant I could slip into my office for a bit. As soon as I shut the door, Sigmond appeared from the air beside my desk.

"Something I can help you with, sir?" he asked immediately.

I walked behind my desk and opened the small refrigerator. There were several bottles of cold water inside, along with a few pieces of fruit, a half-eaten sandwich, and a few containers of applesauce. I'd brought some of this from *Titan* and had yet to eat it.

I took one of the apple sauces, a single deki, and two waters, then shut the door.

"Ah, an early morning snack, is it?" asked Sigmond.

"Not for me," I said, walking towards the door.

"No?" he asked, tilting his hard-light head. "Am I to assume, then, that you're delivering that food to someone else? Perhaps the young man in the next room, who hasn't left the premises in nearly twelve hours?"

"Don't get smart, Siggy. Kid needs to eat or he'll fall over. I'm just making sure he doesn't."

"Might I ask, sir, how did you even know he was still there?"

"It's Freddie," I said simply, and proceeded into the hall.

I left my office and made my way to the medical room. The door was cracked, but the soft glow of the pod leaked into the corridor, almost like a beacon.

As I eased closer to the room, I spotted Freddie in the same chair as before, but he wasn't asleep this time and heard me coming. "Captain?" he asked, even though I was still in the hall.

I nudged my foot between the crack and slid the door open all the way. "Brought you some food," I muttered, walking up to him and releasing the water, fruit, and applesauce cups into his lap. He fidgeted, surprised, and scrambled quickly to keep them from falling.

"Th-thank you," he said, snagging one of the bottles a few centimeters from the floor.

I watched him open the seal and drink it, guzzling the water down so fast, I thought he might choke. He gasped afterwards, then bit hard into the fruit, a stark look of relief on his face.

"Don't starve yourself next time," I said, crossing my arms as I leaned against the wall. "You won't do her any good if you pass out. Then we'd have to put you both in a pod."

He didn't answer but kept on eating. I wondered if the thought of food had even crossed his mind before I put it in front of him.

Petra was fast asleep, but the sudden fuss seemed to wake her, and she cracked her eyes. With a light groan, she turned to see Freddie finishing the fruit in his hand.

"Dressler should be here in a few," I said before the girl could ask what was going on. "She's got something to talk with you about. Something to do with your arm."

"My arm?" she asked, her voice still weak from sleep.

"Don't ask me," I said plainly. "I'm just as clueless as the two of you."

"Here, Petra," said Freddie, peeling the lid off one of the cups.

She smiled and took the applesauce from him. She

sipped the food and I wondered if I should have brought a spoon.

"Oh, wonderful," said a voice from the door. It was Dressler, stepping in from the hall with a large case in her hands. "Everyone's here."

"What's that?" asked Freddie, gawking at the box.

The doctor didn't answer, choosing to instead slam the case on the nearby table. She rolled it towards the front of Petra's pod.

"Doc says she's got something that can help," I explained.

"Help?" asked Petra.

Dressler cracked the lid. "After your incident, I spoke with Athena about something I had discovered in the database regarding human cybernetics. Specifically, limb supplementation. As it happened, the medical ward on *Titan* still had a small number of these in storage." To everyone's surprise, Dressler lifted an actual arm out of the box, its skin matching that of Petra's, exactly the same size as the one she had lost. "Adjustments had to be made, of course, but Athena assured me she could make them within the day. All that remains—" She hoisted the arm against her chest and brought it closer to the pod. "—is to put it on."

Petra's eyes widened at the gift that she'd just been presented with. "Y-you're giving me a new arm? But I—"

Freddie touched her hand with his. "This is incredible! Petra, isn't this amazing? You're going to have a new arm!"

"It won't be the same," said Dressler. "You'll feel the difference, and it will take some time to adjust to the weight and strength differences."

"Like any other prosthetic," I said.

"No," corrected the doctor. "This is different."

She motioned for Petra to ready her shoulder, bringing the end of the arm to her stub. The girl squeezed inside the end of the arm.

Dressler, who was still holding the machine, looked directly into the girl's eyes. "Brace yourself."

Petra looked confused, but only for a second. The arm clenched around her flesh, emitting a strange mechanical sound as it gripped hold of her body. Her eyes widened as the pain hit.

She screamed instantly, pulling back into the pod as her eyes strained. Petra tried to grab the arm to yank it away, when Dressler took her hand and pinned her down. "Hold her!" shouted the doctor to both Freddie and me.

We were quick to do as she said. I took the girl's legs and kept her from kicking, while Freddie relieved Dressler of the hand so she could focus on holding the arm in place. Freddie looked horrified by the way his woman was squirming, but I had to admit this kid knew when to step up and push through the fear.

"Is this supposed to happen?!" I snapped, throwing all my weight on the girl's ankles as she continued to squirm.

"Just a few more seconds," assured Dressler. "It needs to connect to the nerves."

As soon as she said the last word, I heard another clamp inside the arm, causing Petra to jerk away from the shock of it. We held her in place, however, and she settled in short time.

"There we are," said Dressler, still holding the arm but looking more relaxed. "Do you feel anything?"

Petra was breathing heavily, sweat on her forehead. She nodded, licking her dry lips.

"Good," said the doctor. "Try to move it."

Freddie and I let go of her and eased back, giving the two women some space.

Petra's eyes fell on the arm, and she seemed to focus on it for a time, although it felt like a full minute.

Freddie swallowed then opened his mouth to say something, probably out of concern. I anticipated a question about whether the arm was working properly or if maybe we'd missed something in the grafting process, but then—

The index finger on the mechanical hand suddenly twitched.

If we hadn't been watching for it, I expect we would have missed it altogether.

Freddie and I stared with wide-eyed expressions, taking a step closer.

"Again," ordered Dressler to the woman. She held the arm with both her hands. "Anything at all will do."

This time, the finger moved three times the distance as before. It clenched, nearly touching the palm, and returned.

Freddie smiled and gasped at the same time, but still

didn't say anything. He was too transfixed by what was happening.

"Once more," said Dressler.

Petra did as she was told, bending the finger even faster than before. Then, without being prompted, she moved her middle finger, followed by her thumb. In seconds, she had all five fingers bending together, like she'd been doing it all her life.

"Now the wrist," said Dressler.

It took her a few seconds to comply, but she finally managed it. Petra bent her wrist, moving her hand in a circular motion.

Dressler nodded, looking as stoic as ever. If she was excited or proud, she wasn't showing any of it.

She released Petra's arm, letting it fall on her stomach. Freddie flinched as it hit, but Petra raised her other hand to reassure him. With all three of us watching, the girl tried to move the arm. First the fingers, then the wrist, and finally—

Petra managed to lift the artificial arm just above her waist.

"I can feel it," she said, tears seeping out of her tired eyes. "I can feel all of it."

11

We watched Petra continue to use her new prosthetic arm for nearly an hour before I decided to head out. I still had a mission to do today, which meant certain priorities had to be attended to.

I called Freddie and Dressler into the hallway, putting some space between us and the medical room so Petra couldn't overhear us. I wagered the last thing she needed right now was talk of anyone doing another job in the same place she'd just lost her arm. Even with the new one, the trauma of it wouldn't soon be erased.

"I assume this is about the mission involving the drones," said Dressler, walking over to me.

Freddie was right beside her, looking over his shoulder at the medical room's cracked door.

"You assume right," I said. "We need to get this job started. I'll be needing you with me, Doc."

She nodded. "You'll have me."

Freddie shifted his weight from one foot to the other, clearly nervous to ask me what I already knew was coming. "If it's all right with you, Captain, I—"

"Stay here and look after your girl," I interrupted. "That's your assignment today."

He paused briefly, but then smiled. "Right. Thank you."

I smacked his shoulder and motioned for Dressler to follow me. "We'll see you back here tonight, Fred."

The doctor and I left him there, heading straight into the street. As the outer door closed, I heard a voice calling for me. "Captain!" it yelled, pulling my attention.

I spotted Octavia and Abigail walking towards us. They were each wearing their full gear, including a holstered pistol. "Seems the two of you are ready to go," I said as they approached. I purposefully eyed the gun on Abigail's hip. "Where's the rifle?"

"I don't want a repeat of last time," she replied, referring to how cramped the ship had been, making it difficult to draw her rifle.

"Good thinking," I said, then looked at Octavia. "How's the crew? We ready to go?"

"Alphonse and Verne are already there," she told me.

I nodded. We were only taking a single ship this time, which meant the crew had to be limited to only six. Thankfully, I'd already planned on replacing Freddie with Verne ahead of time to give him a chance to rest. Gods knew he needed it. "What about the drones?" I asked.

The comm in my ear clicked. "They can be deployed within a few minutes' time, sir," responded Sigmond. "Simply give the order and it shall be done."

"Wait until we're in the air near the pit," I told him. "I think that's something I'd like to see."

"Engines are primed and ready," said Alphonse once we arrived at the landing pad. He was standing beside the ship, while Verne had taken a seat inside.

"You didn't waste any time," I said, climbing in and taking the pilot's seat.

"I knew you'd want to leave as soon as you arrived," Alphonse replied.

I tossed the mobile emitter onto the dash, allowing Sigmond to appear. "Ah," said the Cognitive, stretching out his arms and giving us a wave. "Good morning to all of you."

"Go ahead and get those drones in position, Siggy. I want them ready the second we arrive."

"Of course, sir," he answered.

"Hello, everyone," said Verne, a hint of nervousness in his voice. He already had his harness locked over his chest but continued to fiddle with the lock.

"Good to see you again," said Abigail, sitting beside him. Dressler and Octavia took the rear row behind them, while Alphonse sat beside me up front.

"I-if you don't mind me asking," began Verne.

"You want to know how Petra is doing," said Octavia.

He nodded.

Dressler pulled her harness down and locked it. "She's doing well, all things considered."

"Really?" he asked.

"Haven't you gone to see her?" asked Octavia.

"One time, but she was asleep," said Verne, somewhat sheepishly.

"She's awake now," said Dressler.

"Doc, aren't you gonna tell him the news?" I asked, placing my hand on the control pad. There was a slight jerk as our thrusters ignited and we lifted off the pad.

Verne looked around the cabin. "News?"

"We attached a new prosthetic," explained Dressler with a seemingly unimpressed tone. "Though it will take a few days before we know if her body will accept the new nerve connections permanently or—"

"There you go again," I interrupted, shaking my head.

Dressler paused before continuing. "Yes, well," she said. "I suppose there is cause for optimism."

"Are you saying she has a new arm?" asked Verne.

"A working one," said Abigail. "I haven't seen it, but Jace says Petra can move her fingers and joints, even feel when she touches something."

His eyes widened. "That's incredible!"

Dressler sighed. "That sort of enthusiasm is why I was less inclined to talk about it. If her body rejects the arm, you'll only be disappointed."

"But if the arm is attached and working, isn't that a good sign?" asked Verne.

"Perhaps," said Dressler. "But it takes a few days for the limb to fully integrate. There is a decent chance her body will reject the prosthetic altogether."

"Stop assuming the worst, Doc," I said, bringing the ship above the city and towards the horizon. "It's not a good look for you."

She scoffed but said nothing.

We reached the ocean quickly, which meant we had a solid hour before we arrived at the chasm. Not a long wait, but it gave me a chance to go over a few things. First, I checked in on the video feed beneath Verdun. Sigmond gave me a quick trilobite headcount, which indicated an additional five of the little terraforming bots had gathered during the night.

Alphonse leaned in to look at the holo image of the growing mob of terraforming machines. "That's concerning," he muttered.

"Worst case scenario, we move to another block," I said.

"Do you think they'll follow?" he asked.

"I don't know," I admitted. "They're only gathering beneath Verdun, and I don't think that's a coincidence.

They must know we're there, somehow."

"Which concerns me even more," said Alphonse.

"Oh?" I asked.

He tapped his chin. "If Dr. Dressler's report is accurate, then the sensors on each of the machines is limited to four meters approximately. For them to somehow sense our presence in Verdun—it begs the question. How?"

Sigmond placed his arms behind his back in a thoughtful manner. "There must be more to their abilities than we first surmised," said the Cognitive.

"Any theories?" I asked the two of them.

"There are two, as far as I can tell," said Alphonse. "Either the trilobites have another sensor that is far more sophisticated than the one we already discovered—"

"Or?" I asked.

He raised his brow. "They're using something else entirely."

Something else?" I asked, looking at Sigmond, then back at him. "What do you mean?"

"A larger sensor, perhaps located somewhere else on the planet. Something that can detect living matter, whether on the surface or on one of the elevated cities. Something we don't know about yet."

"What about outside manipulation?" I asked.

"Manipulation?" repeated Alphonse.

"What if they're being controlled by someone?"

Alphonse was quiet for a moment. "That *is* a possibility."

"You don't agree?" I asked.

He gave a light shrug. "It's impossible to know, isn't it? We don't have the evidence to support any of this, one way or the other."

I nodded. "Guess we'll just have to stay on guard until we find the real answer."

"As always, Captain," agreed Alphonse.

The flight took us across multiple sets of islands, each one resembling the last—an isolated spot of dirt and stone, lifeless and bare. It wasn't until we reached the target continent that I noticed movement on the ground from the occasional wandering trilobite. I wondered what purpose they still had, given the state of the world. The Earth was nothing but a corpse, trying to regrow its flesh, so what good did all these parasites do for it? What reason did they have to still exist?

Whatever the answer might be, I intended to find out.

We reached the chasm to find the drones already waiting in the air. They'd sit there as much we needed before proceeding into the pit, but I didn't plan on waiting very long.

"Go ahead with it," I told Sigmond as soon as we were in viewing distance of the other ships.

"Understood, sir," said the Cognitive. He disappeared from the dash, quickly replaced with a hologram of what we had already mapped of the chasm.

Four red dots appeared above the pit on the holo. "Are those the drones?" asked Abigail.

I turned around. "Siggy's sending them down right now."

"Finally," said Dressler. She pulled out a pad from her pack, illuminating her face with the light from her lap.

"What do you have there?" asked Octavia.

"I had Sigmond relay the same feed to this device," she explained. "If you have a pad, you should be able to receive the feed."

Octavia and Abigail each retrieved one from beneath their seat. "Well, look at that," said Abby.

The first drone dove straight into the pit, blinking as it descended through the first section we'd previously explored. This time, however, Sigmond had full control and knew the route ahead of time, allowing the drone to move much faster, avoiding the walls. It accelerated to nearly four kilometers per hour, according to the readout.

The holo followed it, leaving the others behind and showing the path ahead. After only five minutes, the drone began to decelerate, finally coming to a full stop at the center of the chasm.

"The drone's signal limit is nearly reached," explained Sigmond.

"Activate the repeater," ordered Dressler.

"Right away, Doctor."

A thin red circle formed around the dot, which I took to indicate the repeater had activated.

"The second, third, and fourth probes are en route," said Sigmond.

We watched the first orb remain completely still while the others proceeded into the pit.

Since it was going to take them several minutes to get there, I decided to check out the nearby walls inside the chasm to see whether or not the trilobites were reacting.

The feed swept across the interior, showing dozens of the little machines moving in various directions. None of them seemed to take any notice of the drone, though, which had to be a good sign.

I spotted multiple entry points the trilobites were using to come and go inside the wall, letting them disappear back into the ground whenever they liked. If this mission didn't work, the next one might involve an attempt to manually map those tunnels using some kind of miniature drone, much like what we were doing now. It was something I'd discussed with Dressler and Sigmond but decided against, at least for the time being. It presented its own share of problems, but when you're out of options, you just don't have a choice in the matter.

I shook my head, trying to clear my mind of those concerns. *Wait until the first job falls apart before you start planning the second*, I reminded myself. *Focus on the now.*

The other drones arrived in due time, passing the first and continuing their descent into the darkness. The holo followed the one in the lead, allowing the original red dot to fade away as it reached the peak of the display.

It didn't take the automated machines long to find the place we'd stopped the first time through. I recognized the rockface here as soon as they reached it—the cliff Alphonse had accidentally hit with his ship and displaced the trilobite, along with the spot where Abigail and I had stopped. "Here we go," I said, anticipation filling my chest. "Let's see what's next."

"Proceeding forward," announced Sigmond.

The drones continued filling the holo with new terrain, leaving the previous section behind as they made quick progress. Their speed had slowed, but they were still moving faster than we originally did on our own.

"How long before the second drone has to stop?" I asked.

Before Sigmond could answer, one of the red dots came to a halt, quickly extending a circle around itself on the holo.

"Never mind," I said, leaning back in my chair.

Alphonse sat beside me with his palms on his lap, saying nothing. I caught sight of his thumb bouncing on his wrist, suggesting that he was in deep thought.

"What is it, Al?" I asked him.

He blinked at the sound of his name. "What?"

"I'm asking what you're thinking about," I answered.

He looked at the holo again, his eyes lingering on the two remaining drones. "I was wondering if we should have brought more drones, given the sheer size of this chasm so far, but—" He paused, twisting his lips like he wasn't sure he should say the rest.

"Yeah?" I asked.

"If I recall correctly, the crust is only so deep," he replied. "What happens when we breach the second layer?"

"Petra said something about that last time we were here," I said.

"Thirty kilometers," said Abigail. "That's how deep she claimed it went."

I turned in my chair. "Doc, is that right?"

Without looking up from her pad, Dressler nodded. "According to *Titan*'s records, yes."

"What happens when we're past the crust?" I asked.

"Lots of pressure," said Verne. "You won't want to leave the ship."

"Actually," began Dressler, "there should already be some additional pressure, considering the drones' current depth. Twenty-five kilometers and counting."

"I'm sure they can take it," I said.

"That's not what I mean," she corrected, still staring at the pad in her lap. "Despite their current depth location, sensors detect no additional pressure on any of the drones."

"None at all?" asked Verne.

"It's as though they are still on the surface," she said, obvious surprise in her voice.

"I take it this is unusual," I said.

"It's not just unusual, Captain," she said, finally looking up from the pad. "It simply doesn't make sense."

"Why didn't you notice this the first time we were here?" asked Abigail.

"Frankly, it never occurred to me to check," she admitted.

"There must be a reason for this," said Alphonse. "Perhaps the architecture of the pit is somehow the cause. You did say it could have been designed this way intentionally."

"I suppose I did," said Dressler, looking back down at the monitor.

I examined the holo, watching as the drones continued to scan the interior and build out the map. It took them twenty minutes to reach 100 kilometers, with still no end in sight.

By the time they reached the 500 mark, we'd officially run out.

"I think it might be time to call in a new set," said Alphonse.

I let out a quick sigh, wondering just how far down this damn pit went. "Siggy?"

"Sending an additional ten units, sir," said the Cognitive. "Please stand by."

EIGHTY-SIX DRONES.

That was how many we had to send into the pit before it finally happened.

At a depth of over 6,200 kilometers, the tunnel was totally devoid of any trilobites. Not a single machine resided on the side of the inner wall, nor could the drones detect any of them ahead.

"Wait a moment," said Dressler, examining her pad. We expected her to say something right away, but instead, she only sat there, studying the image.

"What is it?" Abigail finally asked.

Dressler blinked at the question, as though she'd been in a trance. "Oh, I apologize. These readings—they're very unusual."

"How?" asked Verne, looking over his own pad, trying to see what she did.

"I'm picking up Neutronium metal," she said. "But that can't be right. There's too much of it."

I shot a quick glance at Abigail, who returned it. I was pretty sure we were thinking the same thing. Neutronium was the same metal Abby had used to conceal Lex when she first brought her aboard the *Renegade Star*. Normal sensors had a difficult time detecting it, but it was also the one of the rarest types of materials in the galaxy and exceptionally valuable, mostly because the only way you could get it was to synthesize it in an expensive, government-owned lab.

Dressler scoffed at her pad. "That can't be right."

"Doc, speak up for the rest of the class," I told her.

"If these readings are correct, the majority of the tunnel walls are composed entirely of Neutronium metal," she replied. "But that's not—"

"The entire tunnel?" I balked. "Are you trying to mess

with me right now, MaryAnn? We ain't got time for games."

Her eyes snapped up from the pad to meet mine, locking on from across the cabin. "If you would let me finish," she continued, an agitated tone in her voice. "I was going to tell you that the tunnel isn't the end of it."

"What do you mean it's not the end?"

"The Neutronium extends beyond the walls for at least six hundred meters. Beyond that, the drones' sensors become ineffective, but the metal seems to be everywhere."

"How much is there?" asked Abigail.

"I don't know," the doctor admitted. "But it's more than anyone in the galaxy has ever seen."

The holo expanded across the dash, revealing the metal as it was detected, expanding in all directions. The hard stone fell away as the drones entered the next stage of the tunnel, all the jagged edges and small cliffs suddenly gone and replaced by perfectly smooth surfaces.

There were only two drones left at this point, and one of them stopped to extend its repeater. "Sir, the next set of drones will not arrive for sixty-four minutes," informed Sigmond. "They have arrived at *Titan* and will need to be outfitted with their repeaters. I apologize for their delayed construction. I didn't anticipate the size of this chasm."

I sighed and checked the time. "Siggy, show me the feed from below Verdun. You know the one."

"Right away, sir."

In an instant, the holo switched to reveal a pile of trilobites. I didn't have to count them to know there were more than the last time. A lot more. "Godsdammit," I muttered. "Siggy, how many are there?"

"Fifty-one," he answered.

Alphonse's mouth dropped at the sound of the number. It was almost double what we'd counted this morning. I was officially alarmed. "Siggy, I want you to contact Bolin and have him gather everyone in Verdun and take them to the *Galactic Dawn*. Contact Athena and tell her to coordinate with him. Everyone leaves the colony until we get back."

"What's going on?" asked Verne. "Is Verdun in danger?"

I ignored the question. "Siggy, do you hear me?"

"I shall relay your orders, sir," replied the Cognitive. "But I must ask what you intend to do next."

"Move ahead with the plan, Siggy," I answered, touching the control pad with my hand, ready to move the ship again. "We're going back inside, and this time, I mean for it to be the last."

12

We slept in the ship, or tried to anyway.

The ride was smooth, but the anticipation of what lay ahead hovered in the air like a fog. There was just too much we didn't know, and that kind of uncertainty was never good for the mind. It led you to dwell on what might be, rather than what was. All the possibilities tugged at the back of your brain until it became too much, and that was when the panic set in. That was when you lost control.

But with the exception of Verne, I'd spent enough time with this crew to know that they weren't about to buckle under the weight of the unknown. They wouldn't give in to the little voice that begged them to be afraid, because none of us were new to fear. Not anymore.

The ship descended through the pit, passing hundreds of trilobites as they crawled along the rocky interior.

Alphonse leaned his seat back and closed his eyes, falling asleep in only a few minutes. The man was so calm all the time, like nothing in the world could get to him. Could every Constable sleep whenever they chose? Was it some kind of special training or was that just Alphonse?

Whatever the case, I envied him. The only way I could sleep like that was with a bottle of whiskey in my belly, and I certainly didn't have any at the moment.

After another hour, I noticed most of the others had followed, filling the cabin with light snores and heavy breathing. The only exception was Dressler, who continued to stare at her screen, wide-eyed and restless. I wondered how long that would last or if she could sustain that level of energy through the night. The woman's brain couldn't slow down once it got going, so there was a decent chance she wouldn't rest until this job was done and we were back in Verdun. That was the downside of being a genius. Your brain didn't know when to stop working.

I set my comm's channel to go directly to Dressler's. She was only about six meters behind me, but I didn't want to wake the others. "See anything interesting?" I asked, keeping my voice low.

"Not particularly," she muttered.

"Shame," I answered, watching the holo. It showed us passing by another drone. Number thirty-three, to be exact. Only fifty-three more to go.

Alphonse let out a short snort, then licked his lips and turned away.

"Alright, Doc, let's hear it," I said, kicking my feet onto the dash, partially disrupting the holo display. It flickered chaotically before settling.

"Hear what?" she asked.

"I know you've already concocted all sorts of wild theories about what you think is down there," I said. "Including what all that Neutronium is for."

"Do you?" she asked with a smirk. "Interesting. Perhaps you know me too well, Captain."

"I'm a student of people. What can I say?"

"Do you know why the Union created Neutronium in the first place?" she asked.

"No idea," I said honestly. "I know it's good for smuggling kids, though."

"That's one side effect, certainly," she answered.

"But that's not why they created it, is it?"

"No, it isn't," she responded.

An image appeared on the dash, showing a molecule of some kind. "Is this…?"

"Neutronium," she said. "Expertly crafted by Dr. Willard Brim and Dr. Esther Mayweather. Their research has been classified and all attempts at replication have failed. The only means of procuring Neutronium outside of Union control is through illegal salvage operations. The Union refuses to share its research, much like many other military research projects."

Like the cloak I bought for the Star, I thought.

"The material is used, as you said, to assist reconnaissance ships with avoiding enemy detection, particularly when combined with cloaking technology," explained Dressler. "But as I said, this is not its primary function."

"What is?" I asked.

"An energy conductor," she replied. "Specifically, one attuned to slipspace energy waves."

"Slipspace?" I asked, raising my eye. "What are you talking about? Are you saying that metal is good for slip travel?"

"No, not at all," she said, shaking her head. "The ship's plating makes little difference in that. No, what I'm referring to involves the engine."

"The slipspace engine, you mean?"

"Yes," she told me. "Neutronium is a key component in the newer design, particularly those found on larger Union ships, such as the *Galactic Dawn*."

"The *Dawn*'s engine is made of that metal?"

"Only the conductor rod and the associated plugs," she corrected.

"What difference does any of that make?" I asked.

"The metal increases the efficiency of the rod, which creates a more stable access gate, allowing it to remain open for longer than normal."

"That's it?" I asked.

She smirked. "Not at all."

Another image appeared on my display. This time, it was none other than *Titan*.

"Let me guess, *Titan* uses Neutronium too," I said.

"A great deal of it, actually," she added. "It is an essential contributor to its ability to create and manipulate new slip tunnels."

It took me a second to wrap my head around what the doctor was saying. "That's how *Titan* does it? Using Neutronium?"

"That's only one of the components. The rest are still beyond the Union's capabilities to synthesize," answered Dressler. "Though I suspect it may only be a matter of time before they catch up, considering how far they've come in the last few decades." She paused. "All of that being said, my point is that there are two known uses for this synthetic metal, neither of which would make any sense, given what we know about Earth."

"Which means?" I asked, finally turning in my seat to look at her, there in the back of the ship.

"Which means, Captain, that either one of those two reasons are accurate and we are simply missing something," she said, locking eyes with me, "or there is a third purpose to the metal that we are not privy to." She licked her lips. "And right now, I'm trying to decide which of the three is the most likely."

I CRACKED MY EYES, having finally fallen asleep at some point during our descent. Based on the holo, I'd only been out for about two hours, but it felt like a full eight. I was energetic and restless, ready to move.

Too bad we were still inside the godsdamn hole, floating into the darkness. The good news was that we were almost to the last drone.

I checked the holo, examining the walls in the chasm. All I got back was a gray metallic image that never changed. It was all identical—every centimeter of it, with no sign of any trilobite or abnormality.

"Sorry to disappoint," said Alphonse. His voice jarred me, causing me to blink. "You won't find anything out there. Not at this depth. I already looked."

I leaned back and looked at him. "How long have you been awake?"

"Twenty minutes, give or take," he answered with a shrug. "Siggy and I were playing Go."

"Never heard of it," I said.

Alphonse nodded. "Neither had I. It's the oldest board game on Earth, according to *Titan*'s logs."

"I won," commented Sigmond, sounding victorious.

Alphonse smiled. "I came closer to victory than I thought I would, given the opponent."

"You were impressive, Constable," admitted Sigmond.

"Says the Cognitive," replied Alphonse. "A regular marvel of technology and he calls me *impressive*."

I turned to the display again and leaned on my armrest. "Do you think there's an end to this pit?"

Alphonse chuckled. "Based on what Siggy tells me, if

we don't hit the end soon, we're likely to find ourselves coming out the other side, but that would be impossible."

"Oh?" I asked.

The holo display flashed, replacing the image of the wall interior with a map of the chasm. We were at the center of it, tucked between two lines, except the lines were now twisting, curving, and opening up at long last, signaling the end of this long journey.

I sat up in my chair, saying nothing, but waited with cautious breath for the next phase of the tunnel.

Alphonse stared at the display, a gaping expression on his steady face. "Well…every planet has a core," he said, although his tone suggested he wasn't so sure.

The opening widened, and we saw what appeared to be a massive oval, stretching on for several kilometers. No, it was bigger than that, larger than the holo could show us, going beyond what the sensors could detect.

I was about to ask if Sigmond knew where to go from here, when I saw—

Well, they weren't quite walls. Not in the traditional sense.

"Oh, my gods," muttered Abigail, who must have noticed it too. "Are those…buildings?"

"Hanging from the wall," finished Alphonse. "It would seem so."

I gawked at the image on the holo—an expansive cityscape with towers climbing out from the inner ground. They were all around us, like an impossible dream, surrounding the center of this oval from all sides.

This was certainly a first.

"Someone tell me what I'm looking at," I ordered. "Where the hell are we?"

"Ladies and gentlemen," announced Sigmond, this time sending his voice throughout the ship. "Welcome to the center of the Earth."

13

"None of this makes any sense," gawked Dressler, swiping and tapping her pad like a woman possessed. "I don't—why would they—"

"Someone calm her down before she breaks," I said, not bothering to turn around. I was far too busy staring at the display, magnifying different areas of the map to see what I could find. The city—if that was what it was—filled the entire core of the world, every tower and building pointed to the absent center.

All of this was far too large a space to search with just the ship's scanners. We'd have to get closer to pick up everything. "Siggy, how big is this place?"

"I am unable to determine that, sir," he answered. "It goes beyond the ship's scan range."

"Seems we'll have to look around," said Alphonse. He

was calmer than the rest of us on the surface, but I knew better. I could see the worry in his eyes—a hint of something, turning in his mind. Was it fear? No, I didn't think so. Something else, like he was taking everything in.

Studying, assessing, calculating. That was the way of a Constable. I wondered, did he see something I didn't?

Looking out across the city, I wondered if anyone else had found their way here. Was there a Union ship waiting for us in the darkness of this place? Were we walking ourselves into a trap? If only I could see more of the area, I might find my answer.

"How far do the sensors on this ship go?" I asked.

"Approximately one kilometer," informed Dressler, even though the question wasn't directed at her.

"Glad to see you're not hysterical anymore," I replied. "Siggy, is she right?"

"That estimate is correct," answered Sigmond.

"In that case, stay a kilometer away from the nearest wall and hug it all the way around," I ordered. "We'll map the whole damn thing out before we decide where to go."

Sigmond did as I told him, accelerating the ship to cruising speed, monitoring the space around us at all times. Even here, the wall was covered in Neutronium metal, the same as the previous tunnel. Whatever this place was, it wasn't accidental.

Twelve minutes into our search, something beeped on the holo, drawing my attention to a glowing blue set of lines. "Siggy, talk to me," I told him.

"An abnormality in the structure, sir," he replied. "I am still analyzing it."

The object was attached to the lower section of the wall, nearly a kilometer below and ahead of us, right on the edge of our sensor range. It stuck out of the wall like a sore thumb—literally, in fact, now that I looked at it.

"Is that a landing platform?" asked Alphonse before I could ask the exact same question.

"That doesn't mean we should use it," cautioned Verne.

Octavia scoffed. "We didn't come all this way for no reason. Besides, points of interest tend to be located near landing sites."

"Precisely," interjected Dressler. "Which means there's something here to find. Captain?"

"Already on it, Doc," I said, taking control of the ship. I aimed our nose towards the platform and accelerated.

"This place is eerie, isn't it?" asked Alphonse, although the question seemed more like a statement.

He'd get no argument here.

I felt like the smallest fish in the world's biggest fish bowl, except we were alone in the water, no sign of life to be found. It was more than eerie. It was downright spooky.

As we approached the wall, more details filled out on the holo. The area adjacent to the platform opened up, revealing something like a tunnel that extended beyond our sensors. "Looks like we've got our next course," I muttered.

"Look here," said Alphonse, pointing to the holo. He

zoomed in on the opening. "It's too small for the ship. We'll have to go in on foot."

He was right. The rear of the platform came together like a hallway—a width of two meters—before opening back up on the other side. We could try blasting our way through, but gods only knew what effect that might have on the infrastructure. Best not to take a risk like that unless we had to. "Seems that we'll be landing," I said, raising my voice enough for the entire crew to hear me. "Everyone grab your gear and ready your weapons."

"Weapons?" asked Verne.

"Is that a problem?" I asked, turning around.

"I'm not that experienced with firearms," he explained. "I've only had a few hours of training. Most of what I know is academic."

Abigail raised her rifle, slid the chamber open to examine it, then locked it back into place with a hard click. "Everyone has a first time," she said just as Octavia and Dressler were securing their pistols. "With any luck, you won't have to do anything, but—"

Octavia leaned over Verne's shoulder. "You'd better make sure you're ready."

THE PLATFORM WAS MADE of the same Neutronium material as the rest of this place. Smooth and gray—a minimalist design. The light of our ship shined off the metal like a smudged mirror as we unloaded from the vessel, fully armed, wearing our environmental suits.

Despite Sigmond's assurances that there was breathable air down here, I decided to play it safe. For all we knew, this open area was the only place with any oxygen in it. Sensors couldn't tell us what lay ahead, which meant we were walking into the unknown.

The opening in the wall was fifty meters from our position, directly ahead. I was about to start walking, when I noticed something in the corner of my eye.

Verne bounced on one foot, pausing to switch legs and repeat the process. I stared at him in confusion. "What the hell are you doing?"

He looked up at me with a surprised expression, like he hadn't expected the question. "What am I doing?" he repeated. "Isn't it obvious?"

I scoffed then looked at Abigail, who responded with an equally confused look. "Maybe try explaining it," I said, turning back to him.

"Oh, well, we're at the center of the planet, aren't we?" he asked.

"That's what I'm told," I said.

Dressler walked up beside me. "Ah, I see where this is going," she said with a light smirk. "Good observation, Verne."

"What?" I asked, looking at the two of them. "Someone start talking sense."

Verne nervously cleared his throat. "Y-you see, the

center of any planet is said to have near zero gravity. According to my suit, the gravity here is identical to the surface, which as you might have guessed, is most unusual."

"That it is," confirmed Dressler, turning to me. "Not every planet or moon has a working core, which has allowed miners and researchers to dig their way to the middle in search of rare resources. Those expeditions reported lighter gravity and, in some cases, instances of near zero."

"Oh, so that's it," I said, finally getting it.

She nodded. "I suspected this might happen once we observed the lack of pressure inside the previous tunnel, during our descent. It seems the Eternals went through quite a bit of work to ensure this facility remained accessible."

"Facility?" I asked. "Is that what you're calling it?"

"Isn't that what it is?" she asked, motioning to the opening along the far wall. "Every aspect of this place appears intentional, including the landing pad. Whatever lies ahead, rest assured, has been placed there for a reason."

"And what reason do you think that is?" I asked.

"That is a question we share, Captain," said the doctor. "Let us hope we find the answer soon."

14

THE CORRIDOR WAS tight at first but widened soon enough.

There was nothing but the dark ahead, and it seemed to grow as we moved towards it, even despite our own lights. It felt like we were walking into the Underworld.

"I don't like this," muttered Verne. His voice was shaking, and I sensed the fear bubbling inside of him. "I-I don't think it was a good idea for me to come."

"Hold it together," I said, slowing so I was beside him.

His heavy breathing was heard on the comms as sweat beaded down his forehead and cheeks. Kid was gonna lose it if I didn't calm him down.

I switched over to another channel but kept the main one open. I had Sigmond do the same for Verne. "W-what just happened?" asked Verne, noticing the change.

"I had Siggy switch us to another channel. We can hear

the others if anything happens, but for now, they can't hear us. Tell me what's wrong with you, kid."

He hesitated to answer but continued walking. "I-I just don't think I should be here, Captain. This place is… dangerous, isn't it? Look at it."

"I see it just fine," I said, dismissing the fear. "You weren't like this back in the ship. Just what the hell is bothering you all of a sudden? Tell me the truth, Verne. This ain't the time to hold back on me."

"I don't—"

I glared at him with a look that suggested I already knew the bullshit he was about to try on me, and I wasn't having any of it.

He closed his mouth and lowered his eyes, acceptance in his face. "O-okay, then," he said after a few more seconds. "It's going to sound stupid. I know it will."

"There's plenty of stupidity in this crew to go around, Verne. Just speak your truth and get it over with."

He let out a sigh. "Ever since we landed, I've had a strange feeling. Well, more of a memory, I suppose."

"A memory?" I asked.

"Of my sister," he answered. "She died years ago, back when we were kids. I keep thinking about it. There was a quake and one of the tunnels collapsed, taking her with it. I was too young to do anything, but I saw the body after they brought her back."

I didn't say anything as we continued walking through the darkened tunnel.

"They said she didn't die right away," he finally continued. "I used to wonder about that. I tried to imagine what she felt like, being buried in the cold. It used to keep me up at night, and I had nightmares about it for years." He swallowed. "But I haven't thought about it since we left home. Even before that, it only happened every once in a while. Maybe once a year."

"But it's happening now," I said.

He nodded. "Out of nowhere, and I can't suppress it. I keep thinking, this is what it was like. This darkness. This sense of—" He paused. "—of loneliness. I keep thinking how scared she had to be in those last few seconds, and then it scares me." He looked up, into my eyes. "I can't get it out of my head, sir. I'm sorry. I know it doesn't make any sense. I just—"

"Makes perfect sense," I said, cutting him off.

"S-sir?"

"You see that light?" I asked him, already knowing his answer. "The second I saw it, I remembered something too. You ever been to the ocean, Verne?"

He shook his head.

"No, I guess your old world didn't have much in the way of that, did it? Well, I grew up on Epsy, and it had its share of water. Enough you could get lost in it. One day, when I was a kid, I spent a day on a coastal shore, near a place called Pregal, close to where my uncle lived. Pop brought me out there on a whim, all because he'd gotten it into his head that every boy ought to learn how to fish."

Verne looked a little more relaxed, intently listening to the story as we walked.

"Well," I continued, "we spent seven hours riding tiny waves, laughing and making plans we'd never do. Never caught a single fish, wouldn't you know it, but not for lack of trying. My old man brought the wrong bait. Freshwater instead of salt, but we didn't figure that much out until the next day."

I laughed, which made Verne smile.

"All the same, it wasn't so bad. There were worse days with the old man, but that was one of the better ones. I made my way back to the ocean a few more times after that, but that's the day that came to mind before anything else. Why do you reckon that is?"

"I wish I knew," he admitted.

"It's funny," I went on. "Here we are, the sorry lot of us, creeping through the black, buried in a place that shouldn't exist, and our minds are elsewhere, someplace far away. It ain't got nothing to do with any of this, nothing but whatever we can piece together to make the connection, but it's all a bit of nonsense. We're looking to make sense of things however we can, and our minds end up getting lost in themselves. Have you given any thought to Petra since you got here?"

The question seemed to throw him, and he didn't give an answer.

"In all the fear, you've gone and forgotten, haven't you?"

"I, uh," he muttered, his voice trailing.

"Don't sweat it, kid," I said, assuring him. "Happens to all of us. We forget about the world outside our heads sometimes, but you gotta remember why we're all here. All those friends of yours, the folks who came with you from that frozen hell hole—they're held up someplace, waiting on us to give them some good news. If you find yourself in a fog, try to focus on one of them. Think about why you're here."

"Is that what you do?" he asked. "Try to find the thing you carc about and focus on it?"

I looked at the rest of my team, each of them walking ahead of me. I settled my eyes on Abigail then cleared my throat. "Yeah, kid. That's about the sum of it."

We followed the light for nearly ten minutes, never slowing. I hadn't realized how far away it truly was until we were nearly on it, allowing us to see that it was a door.

The only door, as far as we could tell.

It even had a handle.

We stopped before it, perhaps thinking the same thought, until Octavia decided to say it. "I suppose this is all the proof we need to know this facility was built for people." The light from the cracks reflected off her visor, bending through and illuminating her face as she looked at me. "Wouldn't you say?"

I gave her a slow nod then stepped closer and touched the handle.

"Hold on!" snapped Verne.

Abigail and Octavia twisted around to look at him, their hands falling to their holsters, letting instinct take over.

"Easy," I said, calming them before glancing at Verne. "What are you going on about, kid?"

He swallowed. "It's just that there could be a nest on the other side. You know, those things could be waiting for us. It's safe out here, but we can't see ahead. My visor's sensor isn't showing anything."

"That's true," agreed Dressler. "I'm detecting interference."

"What's the cause?" I asked.

She shook her head. "Unknown, but the likeliest is electromagnetic. We should be careful."

Verne took a quick breath. "It could be the nest, like I said before. A machine that creates them, shoves them out like insects from a queen. We could be walking into a trap."

I looked at Abigail, but she didn't seem concerned. Neither did Octavia. They were both prepared for whatever came at us. They'd always been that way. They might not be soldiers, but close enough.

Squeezing the handle, I gave it a slight turn. "Trilobites can't use doors, kid," I said, pulling my pistol free of its holster. "But that doesn't mean we won't be ready for them."

The door eased open, letting the light flood the corridor. My visor darkened instantly, shortening the time I needed to adjust, although I still felt the shock of what I saw before me.

A massive space, filled with towering walls of blinking lights—computers, I had to imagine, placed with such precise symmetry that it almost looked robotic in design.

The area ahead had to be the largest atrium I'd ever seen, with multiple walkways hugging the walls at every level. The ceiling was beyond view, stretching high above us to some unknowable end.

We were speechless at the sight, each of us craning our necks to look as we tried fruitlessly to see the top.

"What is this place?" muttered Abigail, finally breaking the silence. The question lingered in the air as we tried our best to piece together an answer. The truth of the matter was that every step of this journey had been a surprise. Why should this moment be any different?

"I wish I knew," replied Dressler, after a short while, her mouth still slightly agape. "My only guess is that it must be a kind of central processing unit for the entire system."

"Processing unit?" asked Verne.

"The brain of the planet," said Abigail.

Dressler nodded. "In a sense, perhaps, although nothing is certain."

"Nothing is *ever* certain," replied Octavia. "Not when it comes to Earth."

Dressler walked closer to one of the walls, examining

the machines. She was careful not to touch it, although I could see the curiosity building in her eyes.

Abigail trailed away from us, towards a set of stairs. They hugged the wall, leading to another level with a railing. "The way this place is structured…it's almost like a library, isn't it?" she asked, gliding a finger on the silver rail.

"Do you see anything up there?" asked Octavia.

Abigail paused, looking around the atrium. "I see plenty, although I couldn't tell you what any of it is."

"Fair enough," muttered Dressler, still studying the nearby console. Without looking up from it, she swung her satchel around and retrieved a small piece of metal. It appeared to be a thumb drive. "The architecture here is somewhat different from the last time we did this, but it looks compatible."

"What are you doing?" asked Verne.

"I believe I've found an insert," she answered, brushing her finger along the crevice of the slot. She glanced over her shoulder towards me. "Captain, shall I proceed?"

"Go ahead, Doc," I replied, but then added, "Just don't do anything that'll get us all killed."

She turned back. "I'm afraid I can't make any promises."

She plugged the drive directly into the console, taking a step away from the wall and examining the nearby displays, which were still empty.

"Siggy, you in there yet?" I asked after a few seconds had passed.

No answer.

"Are we too far from the drones?" asked Octavia.

"The amount of Neutronium between us and the last drone might be interfering," said Verne.

"He just spoke to us through the suits," said Abigail.

"Maybe the suits are better at relaying the signal," argued Verne.

"I don't think it works like that."

"Quiet, please!" snapped Dressler, leaning in closer to the console, staring at a set of blinking lights. The group went still as a board at the sudden outburst.

All except for me. I just stood there, leaning against the wall with my arms crossed, waiting.

"Look here," muttered Dressler after a bit. She pointed at one of the lights. "This is new. Right here. Look."

I eased up off the wall and walked closer. She seemed to be pointing to a small, constant yellow light. "What about it?"

She held a finger in the air to hush me.

I waited but opened my mouth to ask one more time just what she was talking—

"—paring to restore system and activate interface," said Sigmond with a muffled, static-filled voice. "Stand by for—"

The connection dropped with a soft click, and everyone looked at each other. "What's wrong with him?" asked Verne.

"He's working," assured Abigail. "Isn't that right?"

Dressler stood up and eased back from the console, then nodded, keeping totally quiet.

There was a long silence as we waited for Sigmond to speak again. When he finally did, half of us jumped.

"—tecting internal signature—" Sigmond's voice faded in and out as he spoke. "—ognitive sequence initiating. Protocol override for—" Another pause. "—warning! Trilobite hive appears to be—"

"That's not normal," said Abigail, shuffling down the stairs. "We need to get him out of there before we lose him!"

"Not yet," said Dressler, still calm.

Alphonse was standing to my left. "Did I hear the word Cognitive just now?" he asked, looking at me.

"He also mentioned a trilobite hive," said Octavia.

Right as Abigail marched up to Dressler, the doctor threw another finger up, stopping her.

Abigail glared at it, then at Dressler. "Don't tell me to be quiet, MaryAnn. We almost lost him once before and I refuse to let it—"

At once, a multitude of lights flickered along the surface of the console, drawing everyone's attention forward. It spread to the nearby monitors, causing each of them to fill with different colors, changing rapidly and growing brighter by the second. The lights continued around every wall and across all levels until the entire atrium shined with such brightness that it caused my visor to auto-dim.

Everyone took a step back as Abigail reached for the thumb drive and pulled it from the slot, yanking it free.

The lights disappeared at once, but only for a moment. It was just enough time for Verne to say, "I don't think that's normal."

A flash of blue light appeared between Abigail and Dressler, taking them both by surprise. The two women leapt backwards and shielded their bodies.

Octavia and Alphonse went for their guns, rushing to the forefront, but my pistol was already drawn and aimed.

"Hold your fire, please," came a voice in my ear, speaking to the entire group. It was Sigmond, returned to us, now that the thumb drive had been pulled. "You'll only damage the data module!"

"Siggy, what the hell is going on?!" I barked.

The light swirled in the air before me, taking shape like paint on a canvas. The color came together to form lines and detail, eyes and ears, hair and face, body and clothes. A woman dressed in robes, hair down to her waist, and beautiful.

This was a Cognitive, no doubt in my mind.

"Activating Cognition sequence," said the woman, her voice a strange mix of tones, like multiple people saying the same thing at once. "Warning: partial data degradation detected. Attempting system defragmentation."

"What is this?" asked Abigail, almost in a whisper.

I shot a quick glance to Dressler, who was staring up at the Cognitive with a wide-eyed look on her face. "Doc?"

Dressler blinked. "I-I believe she's attempting to reset herself."

"For what purpose?" asked Octavia.

"Warning: corrupted data modules detected. Unable to restore," continued the Cognitive. "Cognition activation sequence complete with 91 percent restoration."

The woman flickered as the light reformed itself, her shape and body becoming less blurry and more defined. "Greetings," she said at last. "I am the central Cognitive and caretaker of Earth, tasked with overseeing Project Reclamation and all of its terraforming processes. You may call me Gaia."

15

"Another Cognitive," muttered Octavia.

Dressler eased closer to the glowing woman, staring at her with a slack-jawed expression. "Fascinating."

I switched to a private channel. "Siggy, tell me what's going on, and keep it short. Where did this Gaia come from and why wasn't she here before?"

"Apologies, sir," replied Sigmond. "I discovered a series of dormant programs inside the system, including control of the trilobite network itself. Unfortunately, I do not possess the proper authorization, but Gaia does. I attempted to relay this information to you, but when I received no response, I took it upon myself to—"

"Wake her up," I finished. "Right. I guess I can see how that might be of some use to us."

"Based on what I saw in the system, she is the only one who can shut down the trilobites."

Gaia looked at me and smiled. "Your Cognitive is correct," she said, taking me by surprise. I hadn't expected her to hear our conversation. "I alone have the capability to manipulate the terramining processing units."

I switched back to the main team channel. "Did anyone catch that?"

"I think she's talking about the trilobites," said Dressler.

"That so?" I asked.

Gaia raised her hand to one of the screens along the nearby wall, causing an image of one of the trilobites to appear. "The terramining unit known as X201-33SG or, as you have chosen to call it, the trilobite."

"Gaia, what is the purpose of said unit?" asked Dressler, jumping at the chance for more information.

"X201-33SG exists solely to harvest and store matter. Upon its delivery, the material is repurposed towards the terraforming process."

"Just as I thought," muttered Dressler.

"Hey," I snapped. "Skip ahead to the part where she tells us how to shut the damn things down. In case you forgot, Doc, we've got an infestation to deal with."

"Of course," said Dressler, turning back to the Cognitive. "Gaia, how do we disable the X201-33SG units?"

"Simple," replied Gaia. "I need only withdraw the terramining units to their stations to be placed in standby mode. It should be a simple matter of—"

The Cognitive twitched, a digital wave sweeping over her entire body, transforming her clothes from ancient robes to a more modern uniform. Her hair, which had previously fallen to her waist, now hung in a ponytail.

Gaia paused and stared into the air with an almost vacant expression before finally blinking.

I raised my brow. "Siggy, what the hell was that?"

"Unknown, sir," said Sigmond. "Perhaps a malfunction."

"Gaia?" asked Dressler.

"I apologize," said the Cognitive. "What was your request?"

Dressler and I exchanged a look. "I asked how to shut down the terramining machines. You said you might be able to do that for us. Is that right?"

"Did I?" asked Gaia. She tilted her head in confusion. "How strange. I can't seem to recall."

"Uh oh," said Abigail.

"Please allow me to try again. There appears to be a gap in my logs," revealed Gaia.

She paused again, but not for long. At once, a flash of light burst from her body, replacing her clothes with rags, dirt on her hands and bare feet, chains around her wrists. The woman had gone from elegant to disorderly in a matter of seconds. "W-warning!" she exclaimed, eyes wide and unfocused. She looked terrified, almost traumatized. "A-attempted query failed! Unable to—"

A wide blast of blue light exploded from the Cognitive,

sweeping through the atrium. Verne fell back, shielding his face, while the rest of us dove to the floor, unsure about whether or not a Cognitive could actually physically hurt us.

"What just happened?!" blurted out Abigail.

"She must be malfunctioning," responded Dressler, trying to pull herself back to her feet, although she was visibly shaken.

"I believe the doctor is correct," said Sigmond. "The system has degraded over time. It stands to reason Gaia has as well."

"Are we looking at another Hephaestus situation?" I asked.

"I don't believe so, sir," said Sigmond. "Gaia's behavior is quite different. She appears to be having trouble accessing certain faculties, such as certain memories and processes, but her personality remains largely intact. This implies that her basic Cognition is still uncorrupted, which leaves the physical data storage units, such as her capsule."

"In other words, the hardware's to blame," explained Alphonse. "Not the software."

"Correct," said Sigmond.

"How do we fix it?" asked Abigail.

"I might be able to reformat the capsule myself," said Sigmond. "However, you will need to re-insert the drive."

"Do it," I ordered, looking at Dressler.

She nodded, retrieving the small thumb drive and plugging it back inside the port on the wall.

"This may take some time," said Sigmond.

"Do whatever you have to," I told him. "The rest of us will see what we can find."

"The rest of us?" asked Dressler.

I nodded. "I don't know about you, but it feels like someone's pulling the strings here."

"What are you talking about?" asked Octavia.

"Isn't it obvious?" I asked, motioning to where Gaia had been standing. "The way she was acting. As soon as she tried accessing the controls for the trilobites, she lost her shit."

"You think someone did that to her?" asked Dressler.

"Don't you?" I asked like it should be obvious.

Dressler took a moment to think about that. "I don't know, Captain. It could be something as simple as what Alphonse suggested—hardware decay."

"And if he's wrong?" I asked.

She didn't say anything.

"We need to assume the worst. In this case, that means a saboteur. Could be the Union, could be the system. Who the hell knows? We just need to think about every angle."

"In that case, might I make a suggestion?" asked Alphonse.

We all turned to him.

"Gaia mentioned something about there being a trilobite hive somewhere nearby," he continued.

"That's right, she did," said Octavia.

"If we can locate the manual override, we may be able

to bypass Gaia altogether, although I couldn't say where it is," he admitted.

Verne tossed his hands up. "Wait a second! Did all of you forget how dangerous those things are?"

"Siggy," I snapped. "Think you can find us a map before you go diving too far into the system?"

"I believe I can, sir," said the Cognitive. "Excuse me, please."

"While he's doing that, I want us to split into two groups. Doc, Abigail, and Octavia, you three are with me. Al, I want you and Verne to stay here and look after Siggy. If he manages to get Gaia back online, give me a call and we'll come running."

Alphonse nodded. "Will do."

"Uploading cartographer program," informed Sigmond, suddenly. "Stand by, sir."

A map appeared in the corner of my display, along with six red icons, each one indicating a member of the team.

Far away from us, but still within walking distance, another icon appeared. A massive yellow circle with the words "Target Destination" beside it.

"Looks like there's a path near the back of this room," said Abigail.

"Great job, Siggy," I said.

"Thank you, sir," said the Cognitive. "Reentering capsule now."

"Good luck," said Abigail.

"Is anyone going to answer my question?" asked Verne.

"Aren't you even remotely concerned about what those machines can do?"

"That's exactly why you're staying here, Verne," I said, walking to the rear of the atrium, near one of the branching corridors. "Alphonse, don't let him take any unnecessary risks."

The former Constable nodded his agreement.

"Everyone ready?" I asked.

Dressler, Octavia, and Abigail were right behind me, prepared to move out. "And waiting," said Abby.

"Good," I said, turning my eyes forward. "Let's go find ourselves a trilobite nest."

16

The passageway was dark and empty, a far cry from the blinding light of the atrium. If it hadn't been for the suit's flashlight, we probably wouldn't have made it very far.

"Are you certain that Cognitive wasn't just spouting nonsense back there?" asked Abigail. She was right beside me, holding up the rear as Octavia and Dressler took the front.

"I'm not sure of anything," I admitted.

I thumbed the grip of my pistol, trying to feel the groove in it, but failing. The suit's gloves were too thick for that sort of thing—a real shame, since it usually helped to steady my nerves.

"You said earlier that you think there's something else going on down here," she continued. "Why?"

"Don't tell me you don't sense it too," I said.

She gave me a light shrug.

That surprised me. She and I were usually in sync, but apparently not about this.

"Fine, believe what you want," I finally said. "But I've got a sense about this."

"Is that all there is to it?" she asked. "Besides the trilobites under the city and the malfunctioning Cognitive."

I paused, weighing the question, and it took me longer than I cared to admit before I gave an answer. "Maybe, but my head's too busy to break it all down right now."

I could sense her doubt grow, even as I said the words.

She gave another nod but said nothing.

Fine, don't believe me, I thought. *I'm not even sure I believe it myself.*

But that wasn't true either. I did believe, and for good reason.

Brigham had told me to expect them. He'd warned me that something would happen and that I'd have to face the consequences of what I'd done.

An image of the man flashed in my mind. He was in the mud, covered in blood and rain, glaring at me with those bloodshot eyes, a crazed look staring back. A bloodlust that aimed to be quenched, even in death.

The old man had nothing left to lose in that final moment. No cause to lie to me, not anymore. Only the truth would give him peace, the satisfaction of knowing that I'd have to face another enemy sometime down the line.

That was the truth I couldn't tell, not right now in this

awful place. Not to the woman I loved. That moment haunted me, and I knew it would do the same to her if I let it.

We reached the end of the tunnel soon enough. It opened into another room, this one half the size of the atrium. Its walls stretched high, all the same, and a set of wide stairs led to another opening.

We followed the path on the map, staying on our guard and watching the sensors for any sign of movement. The closer we drew to the nest, the more likely we were to see one of the machines.

Atop the stairs, another hallway formed, stretching around a tight corner, heading to the left. We followed it, minding our sides as we passed by several smaller openings. They were mostly empty rooms, but a few had some equipment still inside.

Dressler stopped dead in her tracks, shining a light into one of the rooms. The rest of us paused beside and behind her, waiting for her to say something.

"Something wrong?" asked Abigail.

Dressler held her chest and let out a breath. "I'm so sorry," she said, pointing inside the room. "That scared me half to death."

"Scared you?" asked Octavia, sliding in front of the doctor with her own light as she tried to get a better look.

Abigail and I did the same, stepping closer to the opening. Inside, sitting on top of a large table, three trilobites sat on their backsides, motionless and discolored.

Abigail tensed for a quick second before raising her rifle.

"It's okay," said Dressler, breathing easier than everyone else. "They're not active."

She walked inside the room, towards the machines. I was about to tell her to step away but noticed her hand on her pistol. She was still being cautious, despite her own assurances. I should have expected that, given what she'd been through by now.

Dressler picked up a metallic rod propped up against the wall then nudged one of the trilobites, spinning it around. "Look here," she told us, pointing at the side of the machine with the rod. I noticed a few missing legs and some brown grime caked to the bottom. "These were never finished. Either that or they were being repaired."

"That's a relief," said Octavia.

"Quite," replied Dressler, leaning closer to one of the trilobites. As she did, I noticed her grip the pistol a little tighter. "I wonder if this was where they built them."

"Could be," I said, motioning for her to come into the hallway. "We'll ask Gaia when she's fixed. Let's keep going for now. Still got a job to do."

She nodded then proceeded to follow me. "I suppose we do need to prioritize."

"That's one way of putting it," said Abigail.

The following corridor actually had a few working lights hanging along the walls. They were dim and hardly useful, but the farther we walked, the brighter things became. Eventually, we reached a room with branching paths, one in each direction, three of them well lit.

The map indicated the forward path led to a dead end, so we'd have to take the left one.

The new corridor was bright enough that I could see the walls with some clarity. They were decayed, half-torn at places. That was surprising, considering how pristine the atrium had been, not to mention the rest of the city.

"Careful ahead," I cautioned as we reached the next door. The map showed that we were nearly at our goal, a large chamber five times the size of the atrium, stretching for a quarter kilometer in every direction. "Whatever's on the other side of that, make sure you're ready for it."

The pad right next to the wall was active, so I placed my hand on it, curious to see what might happen. My tattoos lit up with a soft blue glow, indicating they were working, and I waited.

"Do you think it still works?" asked Octavia.

"The tattoos seem to think so," said Abigail.

"That doesn't mean—"

The door slid open like it was in a hurry. I lowered my hand, causing the glow to dim back to normal, and I raised my finger. "Remember how the trilobites react."

"Sound, wasn't it?" asked Octavia.

"Something like that," answered Dressler. "Keep your distance. Five meters. A little more if you can help it, of course."

"We'll definitely try to help it," I said, looking at Abigail and Octavia.

They both nodded.

"What about talking?" I asked.

"Pardon?" asked Dressler, raising her brow.

"If they react to sound, does that mean we can't talk to each other? How do we communicate?"

"That shouldn't be a problem with the suits. They'll muffle your voices significantly. That, combined with the limited range of the trilobites' sensors, should make it safe to talk." She paused. "Of course, if you come across one of them, I would suggest staying as quiet as possible all the same."

"In other words, stay alert," I said.

I motioned for everyone to move forward. Abigail and Octavia readied their rifles, taking positions on either side of the door. I gave Octavia the go-ahead, and she proceeded through the opening, covering the left side, while Abigail took the right.

"Clear," they each said, nearly simultaneously.

I followed right behind them, gun out and ready to kill.

To my surprise, there was nothing. No sign of any trilobites or threats, although I knew better than to lower my guard.

The open area stretched far into the distance, with tall ceilings that must have been forty meters high. Large-scale pillars placed throughout the area seemed to keep everything in place. The only wall I could see was to our left, about a hundred meters away. That was strange, since the human eye could easily see four kilometers on a clear day, and the map said the other end of this place was closer than that.

"Where is everything?" asked Abigail.

"Remember where we are," said Dressler. "This is the core of the planet."

"So?" I asked.

"Line of sight is smaller here," she explained. "Remember the city we saw earlier?"

I thought back to when we first entered the core. The city had been all along the wall, surrounding the open space in the center. "Are you saying we've got limited sight because the ground is curved?" I asked.

"Essentially, yes," she confirmed. "It shouldn't be a problem, though. We can use the map to navigate, and the trilobites are only a threat in close proximity. We can certainly see beyond five meters."

"About a quarter kilometer," said Octavia.

Dressler nodded. "We won't be able to see what lies beyond that, but I don't anticipate any serious problems."

"That doesn't mean there won't be any," I cautioned. "Stay alert."

The manual shutdown station was on the other side of this place, which meant we had a few kilometers' hike ahead of us. Walking in half-blind wasn't exactly ideal, but it couldn't be helped. We had a job to do.

The room—if you wanted to call it that—was almost entirely white, basked in a glow from unseen lights. We passed our first pillar—three meters thick and made from the same Neutronium metal as the rest of the facility. The closer we got to it, the more detail I noticed, particularly the grooves along the upper section of it.

"I thought this was supposed to be a nest," said Octavia after a short while.

"You almost sound disappointed," said Abigail.

Octavia smirked. "I guess I was looking forward to a little action. All things considered, it's been a bit slow since we arrived on Earth."

"Speak for yourself," said Abigail. "I saw enough action on my recent trip to the Deadlands."

"She means the Union thugs who tried to sneak onboard," I added.

"Oh, yes," said Dressler. "I believe I heard something about that."

"Just one of several disruptions," explained Abigail.

"Maybe I'll tag along next time, then," said Octavia, giving her a slight smile.

"Suit yourself," said Abby. "I've already offered Jace the captain's chair, but you're welcome to take it too."

"Everyone, listen," interrupted Dressler, coming to a full stop.

I turned around to see her standing totally still, facing

our left side. Her eyes were obscured by the corner of her visor, so it was hard to tell what she was looking at, but the tone in her voice was unmistakably cautious.

"What is it?" I said in a low voice, stepping beside her.

She opened her mouth but hesitated to answer. After a moment, she raised her finger and pointed towards one of the pillars. "There," she whispered. "Watch there."

I stared at the top of the pillar, waiting, but nothing came. Only the metallic gray, reflecting the room's light. "Are you sure, Doc? I don't see a thing. Could it have been your eyes playing tricks?"

Dressler said nothing, only continued to study the pillar.

She was always difficult to read, harder than the rest, but I knew to take her intuition seriously. I decided to wait with her, along with Abigail and Octavia. We stood there in silence, holding our guns and watching.

Seconds passed, although they felt like an eternity, drenching us in silence.

But I remained, all the same. Watched until my eyes burned. Until I had to blink.

That was when I saw it.

A glimmer of light flickered along the top of the pillar, causing each of us to shift.

I felt a hand on my arm. It was Dressler, although she was still looking straight ahead.

I clenched my pistol, anticipation in my chest.

The indent of the metal broke away, sliding in on itself

and creating an opening. From inside, there was only a shadow—empty at first and shrouded in the dark.

Before anyone could say a word, something appeared from within the hole, twisting and scraping, clawing its way to the surface.

17

It only took a second before a few dozen trilobites emerged from the pillar, each one of them taking a spot along the metallic column for themselves.

Moments later, following the first, every other pillar surrounding us opened its inner compartment and unloaded its own army.

Before we knew it, there were hundreds of them clustered into groups on and around the pillars, like bark on a tree.

Nobody moved, except to breathe. The trilobites seemed to be sitting completely still, like lifeless rocks.

"Twelve meters," whispered Dressler. Her voice was so soft, I almost hadn't heard it.

"What?" asked Abigail.

"There's twelve meters between us and the trilobites,"

said the doctor. "We need to move before they come any closer."

I nodded slowly, then turned to the others and motioned for them to step back from the pillar. We could only get so far away before we started getting closer to the pillar on the opposite side. Sensors indicated the midpoint was twenty meters, enough distance to avoid tipping off the trilobites. "Stay close to me," I told the others as we continued moving.

"Mind your step," suggested Dressler. "Even at this range, if we make any loud noises, it could trigger the machines. Five meters is only an estimate."

"You mean they can still hear us if we're this far away?" asked Abigail.

Dressler shook her head. "I don't know, but do you really want to take that chance?"

"Good point," admitted Abby.

The map showed we still had a full kilometer's hike ahead of us. That wasn't far, all things considered, but we were hardly in the clear.

More trilobites exited their pillars and scurried along the metal, moving along the floor. They didn't stray too far from the columns—only a few meters—but it gave us cause for alarm. Without knowing what they were doing or why, we had to stay on high alert, which meant my finger never left the trigger, and my eyes continued to dart between the machines.

Ten minutes of brisk walking got us to the midpoint,

but then we had to slow. There was a straight line of pillars ahead of us, each one standing about ten meters from the other, and all of them were covered with trilobites.

"You've got to be kidding me," muttered Abigail.

Dressler stared at the line of columns, examining them as they stretched far into the distance. "It doesn't look like we can go around."

"Must be a support beam," said Octavia.

Abigail looked at me. "Any ideas, Jace?"

I thought for a moment, watching one of the trilobites near the floor. I knew if we came any closer, it would react and attack without hesitation.

No, not attack, I reminded myself. *They're not animals. They don't know us from a pile of leaves or a fallen tree. They're just terraforming, like Dressler said.*

I paused at the thought. "Doc," I finally said, turning and drawing her attention. "What happens if we throw a rock and it hits, say, twenty meters away?"

"That's difficult to know," she replied. "I don't have enough facts to make a determination."

"I get that, but humor me, would you? Use that brain and hypothesize."

She paused, but then nodded. "Very well. Let's say you toss a rock and it lands twenty meters from our position. It's unlikely that the impact will result in strong enough vibrations to draw the machines' attention. I can't be certain of anything, mind you, but that would be my best guess."

"Okay, so we don't do that," I said, looking back at the

machines. "We'll just toss it close enough that they can hear it."

"Less than five meters," said Dressler.

I examined the two pillars ahead of us. If we continued, we'd walk right through the middle of them. "We'll draw them to the left and right, between the other sets, exactly five meters from where they are."

"That should work," agreed Dressler.

"Except that we don't have any rocks," added Octavia. "What are we going to use? Our guns? Other equipment?"

She was right. We couldn't spare any of our weapons, and we'd packed light for this trip. Most of the supplies were back on the ship. Well, all except our suits.

I turned to face Abigail and Octavia, popping the seal on my helmet.

Abigail dropped her mouth and reached out her hand at me. "Jace, don't!"

I tapped my ear to let her know I could still hear her, even though I could no longer respond. Without the noise cancelling effect of the suit, I'd have to mind my voice, even at this distance. As Dressler had pointed out, we couldn't afford to take a chance.

I tried to explain my plan with hand gestures.

Throw the helmet at the trilobites, wait for them to move, then head through the center. Everyone understood the gist of it.

Still, we needed a second object, which meant another

helmet. Either that, or I had to start undressing. Luckily, Octavia was already on it.

She broke the seal on her neck and popped the helmet off, taking deep breaths of the open air. Her eyes furrowed, suggesting she was surprised by the smell. I noticed it too, like oil and copper, a strange mix that was only barely detectable.

Could be the trilobites, but who the hell knows? I thought.

With the helmet in one hand and my pistol in the other, I walked to the left of the group, parallel to the line of pillars. Standing there, I shook the helmet at the others, indicating I was ready to throw.

Octavia arrived at her spot, raising her helmet to give her agreement.

Abigail stepped closer to me, concern all over her face, while Dressler only stood there with a vacant expression.

"Ready?" I mouthed, trying not to make a sound. I held up three fingers, then swung my helmet forward and backwards, full extensions.

Octavia nodded. "Three swings and throw. Got it," she confirmed.

I swung the helmet forward and backwards, trying to build momentum. *One*, I counted, when my hand was fully extended.

"Gods," whispered Abigail.

Two, I thought, giving another swing.

I pulled back with the helmet, simultaneously clenching my pistol in my other hand. If things went south, we'd be deep in a pile of trilobites, and I didn't have enough bullets for all of them.

I swallowed, closing my throat as I brought the helmet forward. *Three!*

The helmet flew forward and away in a wide arc. Before it had time to land, I'd already started moving. As I'd expected, Octavia had done the same.

Mine hit the pillar first, right where the metal curved, forcing it to bounce and roll along the floor. In a single moment, the trilobites exploded into a scuttle, each of them moving at the exact same time, like they were one.

Octavia's landed too, and it drew the other side away. They fled to the helmet like a pack of hungry animals, desperate for a slab of fresh meat.

I motioned with my hand for everyone to move, and we ran towards the center, not caring about the sound our feet might make. We couldn't afford to slow down, even for a second.

There was just one problem. "Wait!" snapped Abigail, her voice piercing my ear. I wanted to ask what the hell was so important, but I wasn't the one with the noise-canceling helmet. All I could do was look at her.

She pointed to the nearest pillar in our path, but I didn't see anything.

"What is it?" asked Dressler.

"There's one left," said Abigail.

Octavia grabbed my arm and pointed to where my helmet had rolled. The trilobites were already on it, two of them in the process of mining the metal. We didn't have time for any of this.

"Go," I mouthed, pointing forward. I moved ahead without letting anyone argue otherwise. We had to keep going or all of this would be for nothing.

As I came closer, I managed to catch a glimpse of the trilobite. Abigail had been right. It was on the far side of the pillar, partially obscured by the back half. It was also too close for us to avoid, unless we—

The second group of trilobites caught my eye as they began their return. They would reach their pillar before the first group, which meant we couldn't bank to our right side or risk drawing their attention.

It seemed we had no choice but to make a break for it or risk the ire of the entire swarm.

I dashed forward, the others at my side. We passed through the middle of the two columns a moment before the second group of trilobites arrived at their pillar. The lone trilobite remained in its place at first, much to my surprise, and it looked like we might make it through, until—

The trilobite turned towards us, moving its mandibles as it scuttled forward.

My eyes widened, and I raised my pistol steady in my hand.

The trilobite bolted, sweeping across the floor with unbridled attraction, coming straight at me. There was no choice to it now. I had to act.

"Run!" I barked, and then let loose the bullet.

I fired, hitting the machine's center carapace. It staggered, but only for a second. Another shot, this one to its legs, snapping pieces of them and scattering metal into the air.

I squeezed the trigger one more time. With a loud *crack*, the bullet slammed into the trilobite, breaking through its shell and finally stopping the machine in its path.

But the fight had only just begun.

Sections of the two groups of trilobites reacted to the noise, moving from their positions on the columns to the floor.

I cursed and clenched my teeth. They'd be on us soon.

Abigail swung around as she ran and fired her rifle, spraying metal into the machines. The bullets scattered, since she had to keep looking forward and could hardly get a decent aim. Luckily, it was enough to snag a few, breaking or completely disabling them.

As soon as they stopped, the other machines raced to mount their bodies, instantly liquifying them. The delay only lasted a few seconds, but it was enough to give me a new plan of attack. "Take turns firing!" I shouted. "Octavia, go!"

The horde continued after us, only to be met with a barrage from Octavia's rifle. She struck two in the legs—not enough to stop them—and a third in the eyes, which seemed to do the job.

As I anticipated, the army of trilobites gathered on top

of their fallen comrade and consumed it, granting us a little extra time.

"Two hundred meters!" snapped Dressler. She fired her pistol, hitting one of the drones on her first attempt.

"Nice shot!" I told her, following it with my own.

The herd was gaining on us, even with the kills to slow them. If we didn't find a way out of this soon, they'd overtake us before we managed to kill them all.

"One hundred fifty meters!" relayed Dressler, right as Abigail took her turn with the machines.

We passed pillars on both sides as we ran, each one covered with its own formation of trilobites. I was careful to lead the team far enough away from them to avoid calling too much attention, but I couldn't account for everything. At one point, a few of them must have heard us moving, even at this distance, because they joined in on the chase, running at us from the side.

Octavia caught a glimpse before the rest of us, but rather than say anything, she opted for a more immediate response.

Her shot deflected off the floor, missing the trilobite at first, but then hit the machine's rear half and flipped it over. Another bullet tore through its underbelly completely, causing its companion to go full cannibal on its ass.

"Eighty meters!" informed Dressler.

The wall was quickly coming into view, and soon I saw the break in it, a tall corridor leading to the target.

"Sixty!" yelled the doctor.

Abigail fired, clipping her target before having to reload. "I'm almost out!"

The horde drew closer. I slowed a little, letting all three girls get ahead of me. The nearest trilobite was on my heels, almost leaping at me. I fired at the floor behind me, dropping the machine in an instant. The mob assaulted and consumed the corpse so fast, I hardly saw it.

"Thirty meters!" cried Dressler.

Something touched my heel as I came off the floor. The trilobites were right on us—right on me!

"Fuck!" I growled and fired my pistol into the nearest trilobite until my gun was empty.

The trilobite tumbled as my shots tore it apart, bouncing and tumbling towards us as the horde overtook it. I looked forward to see the opening in the wall directly ahead.

I reached out a hand to Dressler, snapping my fingers at her weapon. "Hand it over!"

She looked surprised at first but did as I said.

I snatched the weapon. "We'll hold them off while you flip that godsdamn switch!"

I holstered my own gun and proceeded to use hers to keep the slaughter going.

Dressler entered the corridor alongside Abigail, followed by Octavia, and then me. "Pull and fire!" I yelled after we'd gone about ten meters. "Give them everything!"

I took a knee, while the two women flanked my sides.

Together, we unleashed a swarm of death at the oncoming army of trilobites as they entered the opening.

The first line collapsed and tore apart as they met our line of sight, while the second wave took to consuming them. This gave us just enough time to target the next batch. It wouldn't hold for long, though. We didn't have the ammunition for it.

When the second line had fallen, I called for everyone to fall back another ten meters. Dressler had already disappeared into another compartment at the end of the hall. I couldn't check the map, but I remembered the switch being straight ahead. If we were lucky, Dressler would already have found it.

I smirked as I fired the last remaining bullet in my magazine. Lucky was one way of putting it. "Octavia!" I shouted, raising my hand in the air. "I'm out!"

She reached down and grabbed her sidearm, then tossed it. "Make it count! That's all you get!" She pressed the trigger on her rifle and continued firing.

I was quick to follow her example.

The trilobites edged their way forward, piling over one another like liquid metal waves in a small sea. I could hardly tell the dead from the living, they were so close together. Dissolved remains pooled beneath them as the others mined the bodies, and still they came at us.

I tightened my left hand around my right, trying to steady my aim, making every remaining shot count.

"I'm out!" cried Octavia.

"Fall back!" I ordered.

Octavia threw her rifle into the trilobites to slow them, but soon retreated to the rear. Abigail stayed a few seconds longer until her magazine emptied, then followed with a weapon toss.

With only me to hold them back, the trilobites advanced much faster.

"Come on, Jace!" shouted Abigail from behind me.

I got to my feet and shuffled backwards, still firing. The horde drew closer, barely slowing as I managed to tag two of them.

I turned and bolted for the rear, the machines at my heels. We had seconds, maybe, before it was all over.

Before we were dead.

Out of bullets, I tossed the pistol to my side. I removed my gloves and tossed those too. If I could strip naked, I'd give them the rest of the suit, but there was nothing left to give. Nothing but my other godsdamn pistol. The same one I'd carried for over a decade.

To hell with that, I thought.

Ahead of me, Abigail was pulling her helmet off. She threw it over my head and into the horde. I heard the visor shatter as it landed, followed by mechanical noises I recognized as the trilobites' liquidation process.

"Get inside the fucking room!" I shouted, waving my hand at the two women.

Their eyes went wide as I drew closer, and together they ran ahead and into the next compartment.

At the same time, I felt a tug on my boot. I didn't have to look to see what it was.

Godsdammit, I thought.

As the plastic material of my boot melted, I felt the exposed air touch my skin. I jerked my foot free of the trilobite's grip, ripping the material from my heel as half of it melted away.

The grab caused me to lean forward, losing my footing in the process. I felt my sense of time slow as I began to fall, the floor coming at me with unavoidable speed. At the same time, the horde was closing in, soon to overtake me. I wouldn't be able to move or pick myself up in time to get away.

This was the end.

I slammed into the floor and slid, shielding my face with my hands and forearms. I heard a scream in the distance, knowing it was Abigail. I rolled from the momentum, allowing me to see the thing that was about to kill me.

The trilobites rushed over my legs, one of them stopping on my chest. Its forehead opened, revealing a small tube, while its underbelly began to glow.

I clenched my jaw, preparing for the inevitable. After all my work and preparation, I'd failed, and it hadn't been the Union or the Sarkonians, but a group of automated machines. Death by trilobites, the tombstone would say. What a crappy way to go.

No, not like this. I refused to be killed this easily, not by a glorified garbage can.

I grabbed hold of the trilobite and tried to pry it from my suit, but the machine had a firm grip on me. It was exactly the same as before, when Petra had lost her arm. The liquification would follow in a moment, and then I'd be gone for sure.

But then something happened. The light on its forehead flickered. It dimmed completely, going dark in seconds. The machine hunched on its legs, although its grip was still too tight to pry.

The other trilobites did the same, all of them shutting down at once. I took this as a sign that I should get up and run, but the weight of the trilobite on my chest made doing so difficult. I tried lifting it with my hands, but it refused to let go of my suit. Instead, I kicked the floor and pushed myself backwards, getting as far from the horde as possible, just in case this was all a fluke.

Abigail and Octavia were by my side again in moments, both of them taking one of my arms and helping me stand. We hustled quickly to the end of the hallway, the trilobite still on my chest, and we moved into the next room.

Dressler was standing at a terminal, a curious, surprised look on her face when she saw us. "I don't suppose I need to ask if it worked."

All three of us were breathing heavily. "Not a moment too soon, Doc," I managed to say, looking down at the trilobite, whose tube was sticking out, mere centimeters from my chin. "Now, if you don't mind, I could use an extra set of hands over here."

18

"What did you find?" I asked as Dressler ripped my suit open, cutting around the trilobite, which I held in place a few centimeters from my chest.

"Aside from the controls?" she asked, not looking up at me as she continued. "I didn't have time to browse the system."

"Well, you have time now," said Octavia.

Dressler cut the final piece of my suit, freeing the machine and fully exposing my second layer of clothes. "Hardly. The only way to break the connection was to power the entire system off."

I tossed the trilobite to my side, letting it clatter and slide into the nearby wall. "Why the hell did you do that?"

She gave me a condescending look.

"Yeah, fine," I relented. "Any chance you can get it back online?"

"Not without reactivating the machines," she said, glancing at the immobilized trilobite. "Normally, I would have searched for the deactivation switch inside the system, but I had to act quickly, which meant cutting the power to the entire system."

"If you cut power, why are the lights still on?" asked Abigail.

"Different system," replied the doctor. "The trilobite network is self-contained. I suspect that's what this facility is." She motioned to the entire room in a broad sweep of her hand.

"There has to be a way," said Octavia.

"Not unless you know the layout of this U.I., not to mention the necessary menu path to deactivate every last trilobite on the network," said Dressler, raising her eye.

"I can't say I do," said Octavia.

"As I thought," said Dressler. She turned to me. "I believe our only recourse is to return to Gaia. Sigmond may have found a way to reactivate her."

"You're the only one who still has a helmet," said Abigail, nodding at her. "Call Alphonse and see what he says."

"Do it on the way," I told her, taking a step towards the exit.

"Agreed," said Octavia. "I've had my fill of this place."

"You said it," said Abigail.

I walked to the hallway to see a mound of motionless trilobites in the center. The pile extended across a third of the corridor, which meant we'd have to climb our way over them to get out.

Fantastic.

I walked up to the trilobites, looked down, and sighed. Their bodies dripped with liquid, so much so that I could see a pool forming beneath them. Somewhere in there, that ooze contained three helmets, some gloves, a couple of rifles, and nearly half a boot.

Had a few more seconds gone by, that list would've included me too.

A slight chill ran down my neck as I placed my foot on one of the machines, holding the wall for leverage.

Dressler, Abigail, and Octavia followed, one after the other. It took us about six minutes to make our way across the metal corpses, and I felt a swell of relief when I placed my foot back on solid ground.

Fuck these machines.

The return hike was faster, possibly because we knew where we were going and didn't have to stay so cautious. More likely, though, was that we just wanted to spend less time surrounded by piles of deadly, terraforming killer robots. Either way, I was eager to check in on Sigmond's progress with the other Cognitive. If anyone could give us a straight answer about what happened down here, I wagered it was her.

I kept a quicker pace than the others, although I

couldn't tell you why. My feet took to their own rhythm, almost automatically. All I could think about was getting answers out of Gaia.

A few hundred meters into the area with the pillars, Abigail hurried to get beside me. "Careful or you'll leave the rest of us behind," she said almost jokingly.

"I'm just in a hurry," I said.

"I don't blame you, but at this pace, your legs will give out before you make it halfway there."

My eyes dropped to my foot and the exposed section of the boot. After a few seconds, I looked up again and sighed. "Fine," I muttered, slowing my pace almost in half.

She smiled. "Much better."

I grunted, saying nothing.

The open section on my chest was cooler than the rest, now that Dressler had torn it open. She'd had no choice, thanks to the trilobite. The only way to get it off was to cut, so cut she had, essentially rendering the suit useless. Not that it mattered much, since I'd also lost my helmet, both gloves, and half my boot. The only reason I didn't toss the rest of it was because I'd been in too much of a hurry to strip.

I stopped walking and unzipped the torso section, pulling my arms out. By the time Dressler and Octavia caught up, I'd thrown the suit on the floor, right beside a group of inactive trilobites.

I strapped my belt on my waist and holstered my empty pistol, breathing easier with the weight off.

It felt good to be free of the extra layer of clothing. The only problem was that the trilobites had eaten through both sets of boots. First, the environmental one, followed by the other pair inside. I decided to toss both sets of boots and go at it barefoot.

We resumed once I was done, and this time at a slower, easier pace.

Not long after I dumped the suit, Dressler jogged up behind us. "Captain, if you would," she said, cracking the visor so we could hear her clearly. "I have a message from Alphonse regarding Gaia. He says that Sigmond's repairs were a success, but they're waiting to bring her online until we return."

"It's about damn time," I grunted.

"Tell him we're on our way," said Abigail.

Dressler nodded, slowing her pace again to match Octavia as she proceeded to send the message.

"Sounds like Siggy was able to make some progress," said Abigail, her voice a little lower as she walked beside me.

My eyes drifted to one of the nearby pillars as we passed it. The trilobites were still stuck to the surface, all the way to the top of the column, even though they'd been deactivated. "I'll just be happy if we can get some answers out of her."

"You think she's intentionally hiding something?" asked Abigail. "We've never known a Cognitive to do that."

I thought about using Hephaestus as an example, but

that was hardly fair. He'd gone through total mental degradation, according to Athena. He'd been operating on his most basic directive, never thinking like a *person*. A normal Cognitive wouldn't be like that, and I knew better than to argue otherwise. "Maybe she's not hiding the truth on purpose. Maybe someone else found a way to break her."

"You still believe there's a saboteur at work here?" she asked.

I nodded. "Every time something goes wrong, someone else is responsible. The Union, the Sarkonians, Hephaestus. There's always a knife at our throats, waiting to make the kill. That's how the universe works."

"And you think that's happening again," she continued.

"I've seen too much of it to think anything else, Abby." I thumbed the butt of my empty pistol in my holster. "I told you before, there's too much going on for it to be a coincidence, and we both know the Union wouldn't sit by and let us alone, not for too long. Somehow, they're responsible. I haven't pieced it all together yet, but I can see the gears in the clock. I know they're responsible."

She was quiet after that, lowering her eyes as we walked. I knew I probably sounded a little crazy, but better that than sorry. You had to keep your eyes open and assume the worst, always looking over your shoulder. Maybe they'd call me paranoid, but to hell with it.

My paranoia would keep the rest of them alive.

19

When we entered the atrium, I noticed a pile of metal sheets and broken parts sitting in the middle of the floor. "That's new," I said, walking over to the two of them.

They were standing near the computer console, little piles of metal behind them. Alphonse, still wearing his suit, gave me an easy nod. "Sigmond suggested we manually extract the corrupted data drives and replace them."

"Replace them?" asked Dressler, walking up behind me. She bent down beside Alphonse and examined the pile. "Where did you pull the new ones?"

Verne answered this time. "There's another control room, not far from here, back inside the city area. It's powered down, but there Sigmond uploaded the coordinates to our map."

"I see," said the doctor. "Do we know if extracting those drives will have a negative impact on the capsule?"

A swirl of gold light appeared suddenly before us, quickly forming the image of a Cognitive we all recognized. "Rest assured, Doctor, that only the nonessentials were moved," replied Sigmond, finally turning to me. He smiled. "Ah, Captain! You've returned at last."

"Siggy," I greeted. "Been busy, have ya?"

"A bit, sir, yes. I'm relieved to say that Gaia is finally operational again, although—" He frowned, looking at the console beside him. "—I was unable to fully restore all of her faculties."

"Even with the replacement parts?" asked Octavia.

"Gaia is missing large segments of her memory, due to corrupted data inside the deteriorated drives. Due to the damage, I am unable to recover all of her memories, though I have made quite the effort."

"Any luck?" I asked.

He smiled. "Oh, yes, sir! Approximately twenty-five percent of the missing information has been restored, I'm proud to say."

"That's it?" asked Abigail.

"You're lucky we got that much," said Alphonse.

"But that hardly seems like enough," she said.

"I assure you, Ms. Pryar, twenty-five percent is quite substantial, all things considered," replied Sigmond. "Would you like me to bring her online?"

I took a step forward. "Hold on, Siggy. Did you find any signs of tampering while you were in there?"

"Tampering, sir?" he asked.

"Did you get the impression that someone sabotaged this Cognitive or her equipment?"

Sigmond tilted his head ever so slightly. "Not that I could find, sir. If you could be more specific, however, I would be more than happy to assist."

I waved my hand at him. "Forget it. Let's just see what she has to say."

"Very well, sir."

The console lights lit up immediately in an array of different colors. Beside Sigmond, a blue cloud began to form, taking shape before us. Gaia's face appeared like a ghost, partially transparent as she took a solidified shape. I watched as her eyes and mouth finally moved, fully animated and alive. She blinked then smiled, looking at each of us as though for the first time. "Greetings. I am the central Cognitive and caretaker of Earth, tasked with overseeing Project Reclamation and all of its terraforming processes. You may call me—"

"Gaia," I finished. "We've had this dance before, lady. Skip ahead to the part where you tell us what the hell happened here and why we just had to shut down your little terraforming death machines."

She tilted her head, looking at Sigmond. "Excuse me, but are you a Cognitive as well?"

"I am indeed," answered Sigmond. "In a manner of speaking, that is."

"Excellent. I'm afraid I do not fully grasp the situation. I would greatly appreciate it if you would transfer the necessary data to me directly." She smiled. "To save time, of course."

"Necessary data?" asked Octavia. "What does she mean?"

Gaia turned to her. "Cognitives can share large sums of information in less time than it would take to say a single sentence. It is far more efficient than having one of you explain the situation."

"I'm not sure if that was an insult or not," commented Abigail.

"I assure you, I meant no disrespect," said Gaia.

I shot a quick glance at Sigmond. "Can you do that?"

He nodded. "I believe so, sir. Please give me a moment."

Sigmond froze briefly in place, flickering for only a moment and finally solidifying. The entire process only took a few seconds.

"Transfer complete," said Sigmond.

Gaia had been motionless the whole time, taking even longer before she moved again. When she did, she had a knowing look on her face. "I see," she finally said, looking directly at me. "So your name is Captain Jace Hughes and we have already met. Is that right?"

I nodded.

"I must apologize for my previous behavior. It seems my faculties are not what they once were. Thank you for seeing to my repairs, all of you."

"We were happy to help," said Alphonse.

"Do you know why you lost your memories?" I asked, hoping for something more than vague responses and ignorance. "There's plenty of folks who'd love to see this place harmed."

"Based on my analysis, I believe the cause is due to environmental exposure, particularly moisture, occurring approximately three hundred and sixty years ago. The capsule is required to compartmentalize any damage, limiting its rate of exposure, thus securing most of my systems, but not without first taking serious damage to my storage drives. A pity, truly, as it also prevented me from fully coming online when the needed activation protocol initiated."

I shifted my weight as she gave the explanation. That basically confirmed what Sigmond had told me earlier—that there had been no sabotage, only natural damage. Still, even hearing it now, I couldn't put the doubt out of my mind. "Is there a chance you're wrong about that?"

"Of course," she said without hesitation. "There is always a chance that the unlikeliest of possibilities is proven true, despite the evidence to the contrary."

Dressler stepped forward, her arms crossed. "If we might table this discussion for a while, I would very much like to ask you a question of my own."

"Of course, Doctor Dressler," said the Cognitive. "I shall try my best to assist you."

"Very well," said the doctor. "First, what exactly is this place? Why is there a city surrounding the core of the world? Is it to coordinate and assist in the terraforming process?"

"All excellent questions. I would be happy to assist you in—"

Gaia froze in place, totally still. The rest of us stood there for several seconds, just staring at her, not knowing what to think. "Uh…hello?" asked Verne. "Gaia?"

"I think you broke her," said Abigail, looking at Dressler.

"Oh, dear," said Sigmond. "It seems she attempted to access her memories again. The problem still does not seem to be fully resolved. I may have declared victory too quickly."

I reached out and swept a finger across Gaia's face, going through her and causing the hard light to collapse and reform. As I lowered my hand, she flashed back into a hardened state, fully formed, and then blinked. "—your inquiry," she finally finished. "Unfortunately, a detailed search has only revealed partial information."

Abigail and I looked at each other, then at Sigmond, both of us with confused looks on our faces.

Sigmond raised his finger. "Gaia, my dear, it seems you are still malfunctioning."

"Malfunctioning?" she asked.

The two Cognitives froze temporarily.

"I see," resumed Gaia. "I must say, this is certainly problematic. A simple search of my files is enough to disrupt my entire matrix. I must apologize, everyone."

"It's okay," said Abigail. "None of this is your fault."

"Well, it might be," said Verne. "She doesn't know what she's done or hasn't done."

"Can you at least tell us how to power on that city out there?" I asked. "Might do us some good to have the lights going."

"Without activating the trilobites, of course," added Abigail.

I nodded. "Right."

"I can do that," said Gaia. "At least, I think I can."

She sounded unsure of herself in a way I'd never seen a Cognitive be—a blank stare and vacant eyes. It was a little too human for my liking. I preferred to have my Cognitives in better working order.

"Should we be concerned about you?" asked Octavia.

"I don't know," said Gaia. "I don't think so. All control actions should be fully functional, despite the gaps in my memory."

I looked at Sigmond, raising my brow. "Is that right?"

He nodded. "Yes, sir."

"It will take several minutes for the process to begin," informed Gaia. "I will need to run a system check and power on the main reactors. Shall I proceed?"

I weighed the options, trying to decide whether we

should let this broken Cognitive follow through with the command or not. With so many gaps in her brain, there was a risk she might break again. At the same time, if she couldn't do something as simple as turn on the damn lights, what good was she?

"Alright, then, Gaia," I conceded. "Let's see what you can do. Siggy, I want you monitoring her, if you can. Don't let her do anything stupid, like blow up the Earth. You follow?"

"Always, sir," replied Sigmond. "Should the planet get destroyed, I shall attempt to warn you a few seconds beforehand. You have my word."

20

We made our way through the outer hall, towards the landing pad where the shuttle was still waiting. All around us, the ancient towers hung like stalactites from the encompassing ground, each one pointing to the center of the empty core.

Abigail activated the door to the shuttle and stepped inside, returning shortly with a fresh environmental suit and a pair of boots in her hands. She placed them near the shuttle door and gave me a look that suggested I'd better get dressed if I knew what was good for me.

I didn't argue. If something went wrong, it would do me well to have the extra protection. Not just the oxygen, but the layer of armor too.

While I was busy getting dressed, Abby went back inside and retrieved a couple of helmets—one for her and one for Octavia. She also managed to grab a couple of sidearms to replace the rifles lost during our skirmish with the trilobites.

I slipped on my gloves and boots, then sealed the helmet, securing the suit. The HUD activated on the visor, showing the facility map as well as the different comm channels available. "Everyone able to hear me?" I asked once we all had our suits secured.

A few thumbs-up and yes sirs.

I sat down on the side of the ship, beneath the doorway. Abigail did the same. She pinched my thigh then motioned at her visor and gave me the sign to switch channels.

When I did, she said, "How's that one feel?"

"Needs to be worn in, I think," I answered with a smirk. "Maybe give it a few jabs. Last one had to take a beating before it felt right."

"I'm sure it will get there." She laughed.

She handed me a fresh set of bullets for my pistol. I smirked and took them, drawing my gun. "Thanks," I said as I reloaded. "I know you probably think I'm crazy for still thinking there's someone coming for us. Hell, you're probably right."

"I don't think that," she said, but kept her eyes on the ground.

"Don't you?" I asked.

"Shall I be honest?" she asked.

"Aren't you always?"

She smiled then nodded. "I think you've spent a lot of

time looking over your shoulder. It's something you're used to doing, something you've had to do in order to survive, and it's a mindset that has kept you alive. It's kept us alive." She motioned to the others, who were talking amongst themselves, oblivious to our conversation. "I would never tell you to stop being who you are, because you have all the right instincts."

"Instincts that were wrong today," I countered.

"Maybe," she admitted. "But you still accomplished the mission. You saved the colony. Does it matter if the one responsible wasn't a human being with ill-intent, but rather a malfunctioning computer system? Either way, you fixed the problem."

I let her words linger, trying to process them. She had a point. The feeling I'd had about something being wrong with this world, something beyond the trilobites gathering beneath our colony, had been right, more or less, but I'd taken it a step further and assumed our enemies had found a way to sabotage us. It had been a leap in logic, beyond instinct or simple reason.

It was nothing short of delusional.

"None of that changes the fact that I was still wrong," I told her. "I assumed something and told myself it was true, and that's the sort of thing that gets you killed." I looked at her. "Gets us all killed."

She swallowed, taking a deep breath, and said nothing.

We sat together in silence for a bit, until the void of our words was so thick, I could hardly stand it.

"I've been having nightmares," I finally continued.

She looked at me, locking eyes, but kept quiet.

"I keep dreaming about when I killed him, about how the glass tore through his face and the final words he said to me."

Her eyes showed her concern. "What words?"

"That the Union would never stop coming for us. For you and Lex. For me. That we would always live with our backs in the corner, fighting everyone just to stay alive. I've tried to put the whole mess out of my head, but then it all comes flooding back in the middle of the night when I'm asleep, and I see that bastard's face, laughing as he bleeds to death. I can't stand it, Abby. I can't stand seeing the ghost I've made for myself. It's driving me crazy and—"

She placed her fingers through mine, squeezing my hand so tight, it went a little numb, and then she smiled. Even through the glare of the helmet, she was the most beautiful thing I'd ever seen in all my life—more than the red and purple dust clouds in the Velos Nebula, more than the green and yellow tunnel walls of slipspace itself, and somehow more than she had been on our first night together, there in the confines of that ancient cave. "Sometimes, when I try to sleep, I see the ghost of my sister," she said at last. "She's ten years old and her name is Clementine. We're together again, walking through the hall on our way to sneak a cookie from the kitchen. She tells me not to be afraid."

"You have a sister?" I asked.

"We called ourselves sisters, even though we were adopted, but in all the ways that mattered, she was mine."

Slight tears formed in her eyes as she spoke, and the weight of her loss was clear. Whoever Clementine had been, she was gone now, only returning in her sister's quiet dreams.

"What do you think it means?" I asked.

"It's a memory," she explained. "A very old one from a time when things were simpler, and we were just two little girls living in an orphanage. Maybe that's why it always feels so real."

I decided not to ask why she'd never mentioned this girl before. Not every secret is hidden because of its value. Sometimes, you just couldn't say it because the pain of doing so was simply too much. I cared too much for Abby to give her that grief.

Instead, I wrapped my arm around her shoulder, pulling her close to me. "Seems like we're both a couple of messed-up scoundrels," I told her.

"Seems like it," she repeated. "But I don't mind it too much."

"No," I whispered, leaning my helmet against hers. "I don't mind that at all."

"ALL SYSTEMS COMING ONLINE in thirty seconds," announced Gaia. Her voice punched through our comm, surprising everyone.

"Since when does she have access to our suits?" asked Verne.

"Apologies, everyone," said Sigmond. "That would be my doing. I am relaying all messages directly to you as Gaia says them."

I eased off the side of the shuttle, plopping my feet onto the metal platform and switching my comm to the main channel. "Let's see what the inside of a planet really looks like."

"Ten seconds," said Gaia.

I walked to the end of the platform, along with the rest of my crew, and stared off into the darkness.

"Five seconds," said Gaia.

"Do you think we'll suddenly see a bunch of scary monsters when the lights turn on?" asked Verne. "You know, like bugs in the kitchen before they run under the refrigerator?"

We didn't have time to answer.

"Initializing," said Gaia.

Beginning in the surrounding architecture, the lights came on in an instant. An entire block of neighboring buildings lit up, casting a wide glow on the walkways and the nearby ground, as well as the platform we were standing on. Half a second later, another block adjacent to the first one followed. The light expanded, block by block, filling out the entire empty sphere one section at a time.

For the first time, we saw towers as big as skyscrapers, jutting out of the ground from kilometers away, their light revealing the true breadth of this place's size. Before, back in the shuttle, we could see a few kilometers, but now, thanks to the light, we could see so much more.

This was truly a city, greater in scope and size than any on the surface. Only now did the true revelation of what we had found finally hit me. "Would you look at that," I muttered, my eyes wide and unblinking.

"Say what you will about the Eternals, but they knew how to build impossible things," remarked Alphonse.

He was right about that. Between Cognitives and trilobites, it was a wonder we were surprised by anything anymore, but here we were, our jaws gaping at a city in the center of a planet.

"System reactivation sequence complete," announced Gaia. "Proceeding with phase two."

"There's a phase two?" asked Verne.

It took me a second to realize what he was asking. Gaia had never mentioned anything else happening after she brought the lights on.

I turned around. "Siggy, what is she talking about?"

"Unknown, sir. She appears to be activating another sequence," he responded.

"Tell her to stop," I ordered, taking a few steps back towards the corridor entrance. "I didn't authorize that!"

"She isn't responding, sir. Please hold while I analyze her system."

"Siggy, I need you to tell me exactly what she's doing," I barked, halfway to the hall.

"Resuming Project Reclamation sequence order zero five," said Gaia. "Activating terraforming protocol thirty-seven."

"Siggy!" I snapped.

"Apologies, sir," returned Sigmond. "From what I can observe, I believe Gaia is initializing the next step in the terraforming process. Activating the lights and restoring power must have inadvertently caused the system to resume its designated assignment."

"What exactly is *the next step*, Sigmond?" asked Dressler.

"I'm afraid I don't know, Doctor," admitted the Cognitive.

I cursed then started jogging through the corridor, towards the atrium. "Whatever happens, we can't let her accidentally reactivate those trilobites!"

"What are you saying, Captain?" asked Verne.

"I'm saying I'll shut her the hell down if I have to," I responded as I ran.

It took me about three minutes to reach the end of the corridor, even at this speed. I swung the door to the atrium open and rushed inside, heading straight for the back half of the room.

Sigmond was standing beside Gaia, who seemed to be totally oblivious to my arrival. She had both her hands in the air, letting them hover like some kind of marionette doll.

"Gaia!" I yelled, nearly out of breath from running in the heavy environmental suit. "Snap the hell out of it!"

"I'm so sorry, sir," said Sigmond. "I fear she's lost to her processes, at least for the time being."

I swept my hand through Gaia, wiping the light particles out of the air, disrupting her face. It reformed immediately, but the empty look remained. "Siggy, I thought I told you to monitor her. Can't you see what she's doing?"

"I can only observe her vital processes within her core program. From that, I can assess the state of her cognition, but not her subroutines, which are currently engaged in outside systems that—"

"What does all of that mean, Siggy?"

"Simply put," he continued, "Gaia has reached into another branch of the system, activating certain processes that go beyond this capsule. Such processes are not a part of her program. Rather, they operate completely independently, with Gaia acting as the external activation key required to turn them on or off."

"You're saying she flipped the switch on something outside of this facility?" asked Alphonse. I'd nearly forgotten that the others could hear every word of this conversation.

"Yes, Mr. Malloy," said Sigmond. "Gaia referenced the terraforming process, if you will recall. This indicates to me that she has activated an outside program related to it. What this specifically entails, I do not know."

"Biome replication process initializing," declared Gaia. "Activating flora distribution sequence in Grid 01, Grid 13, Grid 18, Grid 23, Grid 39, and Grid 64. Estimated time of completion: sixteen minutes and nineteen seconds."

"I think you just got your answer," said Alphonse.

"What's a biome replication process?" I asked.

"The next phase!" snapped Dressler, a hint of excitement in her voice. "She said flora distribution, which suggests plant life. Do you know what this means, Captain?"

"I can guess," I said, imagining little blades of grass popping up from the ground all across the barren wastelands of the surface. "None of that explains why she can't respond to us."

"It can't be from the missing memories," said Verne. "We replaced all of her broken drives."

Sigmond looked at Gaia. "It would seem Gaia is not acting of her own accord, but rather through the will of a pre-established protocol. She has no control over her present actions."

"Can we wake her up?" asked Octavia.

"I would advise against that," cautioned Dressler. "Waking her might disrupt whatever she's controlling, which could result in the entire terraforming process failing."

Sigmond nodded. "Indeed. The best course of action in

this instance may be to do nothing, counterintuitive as it may be."

I felt the urge to do something—grab a stick and beat the shit out of Gaia's capsule—but I steadied myself and tried to do as the others had suggested. A piece of me suspected that all of this was part of someone else's plan to destroy everything we'd fought so hard to build, but I knew that couldn't be. No one was trying to kill us—not right now anyway—and they weren't going to come flying out of the darkness to wrap their hands around our throats.

Brigham's words ran through my mind again, telling me to believe the impossible, telling me I was right to be afraid, but I pushed them all out of my head, and I told myself to be still.

I wouldn't let the dead ruin my life. I wouldn't let a ghost control my fear. Not in this new world.

"Initializing Phase Three," announced Gaia. "Initializing gate sequence: location zero-one-one-eight. Formation imminent."

Sigmond placed a finger on his chin. "Oh, my."

"Siggy? What is it?" I asked, unable to make heads or tails of what Gaia had just said.

He looked at me, a concerned expression forming for the first time since Gaia had gone sideways. "It seems she has activated—"

"Captain!" shouted Octavia, her voice piercing my ear and causing me to cringe.

"What is it?" I asked, tilting my head.

"Something's happening!" she snapped.

"What do you mean?" I asked, looking back at Sigmond. "What is she talking about, Siggy?"

"It's the center of the core," said Octavia. "It looks like a storm is forming. Some kind of lightning!"

"As I was saying, sir," continued Sigmond. "Gaia seems to have activated a slip tunnel somewhere inside the Earth's core."

21

THE CORE CAME alive like a storm as I raced towards the outer platform. Thunder boomed so loudly that I could hear it through the comm.

"How could she form a slip tunnel in here?" asked Octavia.

"Should we get back in the ship?" asked Verne. "*I think we should get back in the ship!*"

"Calm down," said Dressler. "We don't know what this is yet. Besides, an attempt to flee would place us near the event horizon."

I came running out of the hallways and onto the platform, stopping in my tracks when I saw the slip tunnel forming several kilometers above us—above everything, since the entire city encircled it.

The sight of it gave me pause. Purple, green, and

yellow lightning arced across the center of the world, and I couldn't help but wonder if this was the end of everything. Had I done the wrong thing? Had I made a mistake? What was I supposed to do differently?

A massive boom rattled the ground beneath my feet, causing everyone to flinch.

"Why is she doing this?" asked Octavia. "What does a slip tunnel have to do with terraforming the Earth?"

"I don't think that's what this is," said Dressler.

"What do you mean?" asked Abigail.

Dressler shook her head. "Gaia keeps referencing this Project Reclamation. The name implies that whoever built all of this—" She pointed to the nearby city towers. "—planned on coming back. Don't you agree?"

"I suppose that would make sense," said Abigail.

Dressler motioned to the storm. "What if this is how it happens?"

"You're suggesting we're about to be besieged by an army of Eternals," said Alphonse.

"I never said that," said Dressler.

Before they could continue, a flash of light tore through the air, dimming our visors. When I looked back up, I saw the formation of a slip tunnel rift taking shape and expanding, like a knife cutting through an invisible cloth. It grew and bent, taking on a circular shape. It was also expanding very quickly. "Everyone back inside!" I ordered, suddenly aware of our vulnerability.

Nobody argued, following me into the nearby corridor

so that we were just inside, standing behind the metal slabs of the protruding wall.

All we could do was watch as the rift continued to grow, expanding into a massive swirling vortex the size of which we'd never seen. The ground shook, and I caught myself looking at the buildings nearby, wondering if they might crumble to the ground.

But everything maintained, and why shouldn't it? If someone could hollow out a planet's core and build a city around a working slip tunnel, then it only stood to reason they knew how to compensate for a simple quake.

Another flash, followed by a thunderclap, echoed through the city, filling our tunnel with heavy vibrations and dimming our visors again.

In seconds, the rift stabilized into what we all recognized as a slip tunnel, fully formed and pulsating. This had to be the single largest tunnel formation I'd ever seen, although without a proper scanner, it was impossible to know for sure.

"Sigmond!" shouted Dressler. "How large is that tunnel?"

"Approximately thirteen kilometers in diameter," he answered.

Dressler shot a quick look at me. "I think I finally understand what all of the Neutronium metal is for, Captain!"

"What do you mean?" I asked, almost shouting as I tried to speak above the sound of the storm.

"A tunnel that size shouldn't be possible. The largest on record is only nine kilometers, and it was only opened once. The Neutronium must be acting as a conduit for the slipspace engine. That's the only explanation that makes any sense."

"If that's true, then we're not just standing in a city," said Alphonse. "We're inside the engine itself!"

"Sir," interrupted Sigmond. "With your permission, I'd like to suggest a deep scan of the tunnel using one of the drones."

"Won't that break your link to the surface?" I asked.

"In the time we have been here, I've sent an additional fifteen drones through the outer chasm. They are currently hovering near the lowest point, above the core entrance."

"So how's that gonna work, Siggy? You shoot a few of them inside that thing?" I asked.

"Is that a good idea?" asked Verne.

"If this tunnel operates the same as any other slipspace rift, it shouldn't be a problem," said Alphonse. He looked at Dressler for confirmation, and she gave a simple nod.

"Sounds like you have the go-ahead, Siggy," I told him.

"Before you start," interjected Dressler, "could you forward the drone's video feed to us?"

"Yes, Doctor. Proceeding now," said the Cognitive.

A livestream appeared in the corner of my visor, showing the lowest point in the outer chasm as the drone drifted from its resting position and into the open core. By its own perspective, the slip tunnel looked like it was floating high above it. I'd already forgotten that no matter where you were inside this place, the center was always *Up*.

The drone thrusted forward, towards the rift. At the same time, I could see a small light moving against the city's backdrop, headed to the center of the core.

"Sigmond, how is Gaia doing right now?" asked Dressler. "Is she still in a trance?"

Another feed appeared in the opposite corner of our visors, showing Gaia in the same position as before. She was almost frozen in place. "I'm afraid so, Doctor," answered Sigmond.

"In that case, we have no choice but to proceed," said Dressler. "Wouldn't you say, Captain?"

"I would," I replied. "Siggy, let's head inside. Keep the drone's sensors running at all times and relay every ounce of data to the other drones so we can analyze it later."

"Understood, sir," said Sigmond.

The drone pressed forward, closing the gap between itself and the rift. The swirling nexus of the event horizon shined with familiar green shades of color. Aside from the sheer size of it, this tunnel was identical to all the others I'd come across in my travels, which meant we probably had little to fear from it, at least from this far away.

Then again, nothing about this place was normal, so I couldn't bet on anything just yet.

The drone entered the rift, diving into the enormous vortex like a flea diving into a pond. I watched the feed as it quickly distorted into a garbled mess of an image, breaking and fragmenting until it was indecipherable, finally going completely black.

"That didn't last long," said Abigail.

"There's too much interference," said Dressler.

"The image is gone," interjected Sigmond. "However, the scans are still populating. I am receiving them now and relaying them to *Titan* for Athena's analysis. The drone's signal is diminishing by the second, but—"

The rift flashed with a sudden bolt of lightning, taking us all by surprise. From inside, a solid object appeared, growing as it bulged from within the vortex, expanding into our reality. It was metallic and gray, rectangular in design—at least, at first. A moment later, another section of it emerged, diagonal from the first, giving the object a shape not unlike a sideways Y.

"What the hell is that?!" I balked.

"Is it a ship?" asked Verne.

"What else could it be?" asked Octavia.

"Siggy, get another drone close to it, quick!" I ordered.

Before I could even finish the sentence, a video feed appeared on my display, showing another drone moving from inside the chasm, towards the middle of the rift. In less than ten seconds, we had an up close and personal view of the object, but it still wasn't enough to definitively say what we were looking at.

The object continued to move its way out of the tunnel and into the open air. I expected there to be more to it, like thrusters near the rear, or perhaps another section.

Instead, the drone accelerated above and around the object, giving us a closer look at the whole of it, revealing a broken section near the rear, severed in two with debris floating all around it. A snapshot glimpse showed multiple layers inside the open, sundered area, pieces of furniture and—

Verne made an audible squeamish noise, raising his arm over his visor as three corpses floated near the aft section of the Y-shaped vessel. They were albinos, with white hair and strange clothes—red and black uniforms, by the look of them.

"Are those Eternals?" whispered Abigail, unable to hide the shock in her voice.

Dressler pushed herself up from her crouched position. "Sigmond," she said hurriedly.

"Yes, Doctor."

"Can you calculate the trajectory of that ship once it's free of the tunnel?" she asked.

Everyone looked at her, but no one said a word.

"Processing," said Sigmond. "Based on current momentum, gravity distribution inside the core, and the shape of the craft, I estimate a probability of 98.7 percent that the vessel will crash here."

The map pulled out and a small section lit up in red to indicate what was about to become a very large crash site.

And we happened to be standing right on top of it.

"Everyone get to the ship!" I shouted, leaping to my feet.

Abigail and Alphonse were the first ones out of the corridor, followed by Dressler and Octavia. Verne lagged behind them, fumbling with his weapon as he tried to keep up.

I hooked my hand around his arm and jerked him into a run. "I said move, godsdammit!"

Right at that moment, the feed from the drone showed the rift suddenly close, evaporating into thin air the same way it had appeared, wide sparks of green lightning lingering in the air for a few seconds longer.

Sigmond had the ship's engines primed as soon as we were at the door, filing inside as quickly as our bulky suits would let us. I squeezed up front with Alphonse and, without waiting for the door to close, placed my hand on the control pad and brought us off the ground.

The object from the rift dipped towards us. It moved slowly at first, but then began to dive, accelerating by the second as it plunged to our position.

Our thrusters ignited into a full blast, taking us away from the platform with such speed that I felt myself press into my chair. Unable to move from the acceleration, I caught the other ship out of the corner of my eye, spiraling to the place we'd just left.

I watched the crash from the drone's perspective, magnified from a distance, but it was catastrophic. The vessel slammed into four large towers, breaking them apart like sandcastles while still maintaining the ship's basic shape until it finally struck the ground.

Waves of orange fire swept across the cityscape in apocalyptic fashion, consuming everything. Dust blew into the air so high above the ground that it dwarfed the towers below. Thick clouds extended far into the open air of the core, floating and forming a hue of gray shine as the fire's light danced within.

I could hardly believe it. The atrium. A sixth of the city. All of it destroyed, along with the ship and the Eternals it carried.

Except…

"Sir," said Sigmond, breaking my attention. "I believe I have something else you may want to see."

"What is it?" I asked, still transfixed on the mass destruction of the crash.

"I'm detecting multiple ships across the city, each one originating from inside the crashed vessel."

"Inside?" I asked. "Are you talking about escape pods?"

"Unknown, sir, but that does seem likely."

"Escape pods?" asked Verne. "What do we do?"

Abigail looked at him like he was stupid. "What do you think?"

Alphonse nodded. "No matter their intent, we need to control the situation, which means gathering survivors and questioning them."

He was right. Even if they turned out to be our enemy, we couldn't let them go about their own business. For all any of us knew, there was a superweapon somewhere down here, and these people knew the key to activating it. Hell, they might even try to reactivate the trilobites, and I sure as hell wasn't having that again.

"Siggy, pull the rest of those spare drones you brought," I ordered. "Have them monitor all of the pods and any survivors. If it moves, I want it tracked. Understand?"

"Yes, sir," said Sigmond.

"In the meantime, get Athena on the line and tell her to send us a batch of ships, and get a security squad on each of them. Their job is to find anyone lucky enough to survive this mess."

"What about us? What are we doing?" asked Verne.

"We're already here, ain't we?" I asked, cocking my head as I sent a command to our ship, ordering it to head to the nearest escape pod. "Let's find out who these folks are and what they mean to do."

22

THE FIRST POD we came to was also the biggest, according to our sensors. It was at least the size of the strike ship, if not a few meters bigger.

Smoke rose from where the pod had landed, having torn through a small building, leaving small fires in its trail. The same was true of all the rest, each of them finding the ground in a less than ideal trajectory.

I told myself it couldn't be helped. Anyone with control over their ship wouldn't bring it down like that, not if they valued their own lives.

There wasn't any room for me to land, so I had to hover over a leveled section of the path. We opened the side of our ship and lowered the ladder, and I took the lead.

"Abigail and Octavia, you two are with me," I ordered,

deciding it would be better to have my best guns beside me should anything go wrong.

"What about me?" asked Dressler. "I understand you need Alphonse to fly the ship, but I would prefer to go."

"Sorry, Doc. Your skill ain't with a gun," I told her unapologetically. "Things go south, I need you and that brain of yours to find a way to fix all this."

"Do I need to ask why I'm not going?" asked Verne, slouching in his seat.

Abigail gave him a pat on the shoulder. "Baby steps. You did well today."

Verne smiled at the compliment.

I climbed down a few rungs on the ladder, looking up at Alphonse, who had taken my seat at the helm. "Hey, Al, make sure you keep an eye on whoever comes out of that ship."

He nodded.

"I'm serious, Al. Don't you let me get shot, you hear me?"

I lowered myself down to the last rung in the ladder and hopped to the ground, followed shortly by Abigail, and then Octavia.

Abigail drew a rifle from her back, which Verne had been kind enough to give her, since she'd lost the other one to the trilobites. "Do you think these people are real Eternals?" she asked, checking the magazine and safety. "They could be similar to Verne and Karin."

"Maybe," I said, unholstering my pistol. I pulled the hammer back, readying myself. "Can't know from looking at 'em. We'll have to have ourselves a nice long chat."

"Hopefully, without all the shooting," said Octavia, drawing her weapon.

I pressed forward, minding my step along the rough and broken path. It had, only a short while ago, been so pristine—sleek and almost new, with a metallic surface that was near kingly in its design. Now all that remained was a stark contrast—ugly and cruel, a nightmare of crumbling buildings and smoke. If not for our suits, I wagered we'd be coughing our lungs out at this very moment.

Alphonse kept the ship above and behind us, giving him a bird's eye view of the situation. It was the perfect view for cover fire, should things get out of hand.

I hoped that didn't happen, not for my own sake, but for theirs. These Eternals, for all their power and strength, were in no position to make demands.

The camera on my suit fed what I saw directly to Sigmond, who ran an analysis on the pod. He lit up a small square of red light, marking it. "I believe that is the manual release, sir."

"Good job, Siggy," I told him, then waved at the girls to step clear and watch my back. They readied themselves behind a collapsed wall, placing their guns on the broken metal slabs.

I touched the ship at the place where Sigmond had

indicated, and my tattoos lit up, causing the lid to flip open. Inside, a single handle waited. I took it, pulled, and turned.

There was a loud *POP* as the door snapped free of the wall and fell onto the ground beside me. I backed up quickly and raised my pistol.

Inside the opening, I saw shadows moving against a white light, vapor and smoke floating through them.

Whoever was in there, they were still alive.

I tried to swallow but found my throat too dry. I took a quick breath and edged closer to the ship again, making sure to keep my pistol aimed at whatever lay inside.

I deactivated my suit's sound filter and cleared my throat. "Whoever's in there, come out! Keep your hands where I can see them!"

I waited, tempted to get even closer, but remained in place. They'd have to eventually come out, and if they didn't, I had a ship behind me to see that they did.

"We have your ship surrounded!" I shouted. "We don't mean you any harm. We just need to see who you are and ask you some questions!"

The shadows continued to move, but there was no answer. I glanced back at Abigail, then again at the doorway.

"If you refuse to come outside, we have a ship that'll blow a hole twice the size of this door," I cautioned. "You wanna risk dying out of sheer stubbornness?"

"Akka le no sing!" called a voice from inside the ship.

I stiffened, looking again at Abigail. Her eyes were wider than I'd ever seen them. *Holy shit*, I mouthed.

She nodded, slowly, her mouth agape, and then looked again at the door.

"Say again!" I shouted.

"Boki na finke sri la!" the voice yelled back.

I switched over to the comm. "Doc, tell me you're hearing this."

"I am, but I don't know what they're saying. Verne says he doesn't understand it either," explained Dressler.

"Don't we have one of those translator devices?" asked Octavia.

"Pardon me, sir, but I've already been working on decoding the language," said Sigmond. "The cipher is processing it now, but it requires more of the language."

"Guess that means we need to get them talking," I muttered, then flipped the comm off and took a breath. "Hey! Say something else!"

"Eddi na kalo? So bicki de rei!"

"A little more, sir," said Sigmond.

"Shudo mal broken, odsi na help! We have no suddala for the wounded! Please stay your weapon!"

"I believe the translator is functioning, sir," informed Sigmond. "Speak when ready and they should be able to understand."

"Did you just say something about wounded?" I yelled.

"Yes!" exclaimed a male voice from inside the ship. "Yes! Do you understand me? Please, if you do, don't shoot us! We mean you no harm, but we have wounded and require medical attention immediately!"

I flipped my comm back on then looked at Octavia and Abby. "It's a small ship for all of us, plus their crew. If a fight breaks out, I'll come running out, so I need the two of you to stay here and gun down anyone that chases me. I'll give you a shout if it looks like it's going that way."

They both nodded.

I glanced up at the ship. "Get all that, Al?"

"Loud and clear, Captain," he replied. "Steady hands and mindful eyes."

I grabbed hold of the side of the doorway, propping myself up but still making sure to keep my pistol free and ready.

As soon as my feet were planted, I was met by a man's face a few meters ahead of me. He had both his hands raised, was dressed in a red and black uniform, and looked almost identical to the other albinos—white hair, blue eyes, and pale skin.

He also looked absolutely terrified.

"Please, whoever you are, we need help," said the stranger in front of me. He looked at the gun in my hand and swallowed.

"First, you're going to tell me who the hell you are and

why you just crashed your godsdamn ship into my planet," I told him.

"There's no time!" he blurted out. He stepped to his side and planted his back against the wall, motioning to the rear of the ship at a woman lying on the floor. "Rika needs medical attention at once! Please!"

I stared at Rika's strained face. Beads of sweat slid across her cheeks and forehead, no doubt from the gaping piece of metal sticking through the side of her gut.

I decided to take a chance and help her, finally holstering my pistol. I looked directly at the man in front of me and said, "Try anything and the ship outside blows us all to Hell. You understand me, pal?"

He nodded quickly, clasping his hands together. "Whatever you say!"

"Siggy, send all of this to Dressler and the others. If any of you see something, tell me," I ordered, walking quickly to the other side of the ship. "Octavia, get your ass to the back of the ship and cover me. Keep your distance, though."

"On it," she replied.

I checked over the girl but didn't touch her. There were several other people standing or sitting around her, all of them terrified. In the corner, near a torn open storage closet, lay the body of a small boy. I tried not to look at him.

Once Octavia was inside, I took a step away from the woman, positioning myself so I could clearly see everyone in the cabin. "Alright, Octavia. You still got your med pack?"

"I do," she answered.

"Get over here and see to the girl," I ordered. "Abby, take Octavia's spot at the door. Keep your eyes open."

They both did as I told them, taking their second positions while I watched the Eternals.

Octavia bent down near the injured woman and retrieved a small box on her hip. She gave Rika a gentle smile and said, "Try to relax. Understand?"

Rika nodded, her whole body shaking.

I motioned at the man who had answered my first call to come closer. When he was about a meter from me, I held out a hand to stop him. "That's good right there," I told him. "What's your name?"

"I'm Leif Wisand, Second Lieutenant to the third Chair," he explained. "And before you ask, it wasn't our intention to come here, I must assure you. It was the opposite, in fact."

"What are you talking about?" I asked.

"Our team was stationed near the gateway for the time when the homeworld would reactivate the path. We've been monitoring slipspace activity for centuries, always on the run and in the dark. Truthfully, we didn't know if this gate was even the right one. We—"

"Leif, you're gonna have to slow down and start making sense," I interrupted. "From my end, I don't know who you are or why you're here. I just know you came barreling through that slip tunnel on a busted-ass ship that—"

"A space station," he corrected.

"A what?" I asked.

"The ship you saw when we arrived was our station," he explained. "As I said, we were studying the gateway, hoping to find a means of opening it to follow the path home. It's all we've wanted for nearly a thousand years."

"Captain, might I have a word with this man?" asked Dressler, her voice breaking in through the comm.

"By all means, Doc," I said. "Siggy, put her through."

Leif looked confused by my response, so I fanned a hand at him. "Got a friend who wants to talk," I assured him. "Go ahead, Doc."

"Hello, Leif," said Dressler, her voice coming through the suit's speaker device. "Can you hear me?"

He nodded.

"Excellent," she replied. "From what you've said, it sounds like your arrival was an accident. Is this correct?"

"Yes," answered Leif. "The gateway was far larger than we anticipated. Every other known gate is a fraction of the size, and we believed we were far enough away to avoid direct contact, but—" He looked at Rika and shook his head. "—Clearly, we were wrong."

"Their station must have been partially inside the event horizon when it formed," explained Dressler.

"That right, Leif?" I asked.

"I believe so," he confirmed.

Dressler continued. "You were saying something about always running and living in the dark. What did you mean? Can you elaborate?"

His breathing seemed to quicken when he heard the words. "Y-yes, I'll tell you everything, but I fear we have little time to spare."

"What does that mean?" I asked. "Little time until what?"

"Until they come for us," he warned. "Come for all of us, yourselves included, and this world you've inherited. Everything. They'll kill us all to have it!"

His eyes were wide with fear now, blood pumping as the words left him. It had been some time since I saw fear that heavy on a man's face, and I knew better than to ignore it.

"Who are you talking about?" I asked him, finally lowering my gun. "Who's after your people?"

"A race of evolved Eternals intent on wiping the rest of us from the galaxy," said Leif.

"Evolved?" repeated Dressler.

"Forced evolution through genetic engineering," explained Leif. "They are unlike anything you've ever seen. We have no means of combating them. Our only recourse was to find the gate back to this world and shut it down from the other side."

Octavia looked up at me, drawn by what this man was saying. "Who are these people?" she asked.

"We call them the Brine, but only out of malice. The

name they give themselves is too arrogant, so we actively avoid it."

"Still, I'd like to hear it," said Dressler.

Leif took a breath, his lip twitching as he did. He slowly steadied himself, looked me directly in the eye, and said, "They call themselves the Celestials, and please, for all our sakes, help us close the gate. Help us lock them out!"

EPILOGUE

I ordered every ship to evacuate the survivors to the surface, letting Athena coordinate the move. The whole process would take days, but I was confident we'd get everything handled by the time it was all over.

I also had everyone on the *Dawn* return to Verdun, now that we'd taken care of the trilobite infestation. As it turned out, every single mechanical bug on the planet had stopped working at the exact moment we'd pulled the plug. Shortly after that, several new facilities had emerged from underground, each of them shaped like large domes and containing countless storage lockers and cryogenically frozen bio-specimens. At least, that was how Sigmond had described them.

I was more concerned with our new friends and their warnings of an impending threat from across the galaxy. If what Leif had told me was right, we were going to have our hands full with more than just a few hundred domes and some new refugees.

That was why I needed every ounce of intelligence I could find, which meant we'd have to question Leif again, along with most of the other survivors. It also meant analyzing the data we'd collected so far, including the long-range scans from the drone we lost inside the slip tunnel.

I sat in my office, leaned back in my chair, and stared at the holo image hovering over my desk. Alphonse and Sigmond were right beside me. I would've had the rest of the crew here for this, but they were all busy handling the mess outside. For now, the three of us would have to do, and I reckoned that was enough.

The image before me was a nebula. Large, mostly pink and white, with a breadth of stars around and within. I'd never seen it before, but the drone had sent it back, along with a few thousand other images from inside the tunnel that revealed nothing.

"The ancients called this place the Eagle Nebula," said Sigmond. "This particular grid was known as the Pillars of Creation. The gas and dust are in the process of creating new stars, hence its name."

"I'm not familiar with this one," said Alphonse.

"That is because it is located approximately seven thousand light years from Earth," said the Cognitive. "It is, however, two light years from the slip tunnel's exit point."

"Do you think this is where the Celestials are?" I asked.

"We have little data to support any current hypothesis, but I believe this nebula contains enough resources and renewable energy to power such a civilization," said Sigmond.

I leaned forward, staring at the floating nebula on my desk. "What do you think, Al?"

"What about?" he asked.

"This so-called threat," I answered, cocking my brow. "You're the Constable. Tell me the truth. Is this something we can handle?"

"Honestly, I don't know, but there are factors to consider before we make any decisions," he explained.

"Such as?" I asked.

He tipped his hand. "If these so-called Celestials have guided their own evolution, what exactly does that entail? How much more sophisticated is their biology compared to the Eternals? Overspecialization leads to weakness, so are they more adapted to an oxygenated atmosphere, or can they somehow exist in other places, such as space? Do they even *breathe*?" He tapped his chin thoughtfully and took a few steps away from the desk towards the door. "For that matter, with easy access to infinite basic materials in the nebula, can they be defeated through a war of attrition? Our resources are not limitless, but theirs might be. We know their ancestors were capable of creating Cognitives and drone fleets. Did they continue to perfect their drone and Cognitive technology even further?" He swung back around to face me, pulling his sleeve back to reveal one of his blue tattoos. "The Eternals developed *these* to act as a universal access key to interface with their technology. What could the Celestials have built that improves upon this idea? Is there something else entirely that they have developed that makes it obsolete?"

I stared at him, momentarily dumbstruck. "Damn, Al. Did you *just* think of all that?"

He smirked. "The first few came to me earlier, during our talk with Leif, but the rest followed once I started going." He shook his head. "Truthfully, Captain, it does seem an overwhelming task, I must admit, but so were all the others. The Union, the Sarkonians, Hephaestus, and the drones. More recently, the trilobites."

"It never ends, does it?" I asked with a sigh. "We've gone through all manner of hell."

"Yes," he said, leaning onto the side of my desk and looking me in the eye. "And yet, here we are."

I let my eyes drift to the holo, staring at the brightest star in the pink nebula. "Here we are," I muttered, letting my friend's words settle in my mind.

I'd come all this way, brought these people together, found us a home. Through everything, we'd never given up, never chose to turn and run from any of it.

I imagined Brigham in the mud again, threatening me, even as the life drained from his body. He'd told me that the enemy would always be after us, that I'd always be running and fighting to survive. Maybe he was right. Maybe that was simply my role in the universe and I was destined to bleed and kill until the day I fell.

If that was true, then so be it. I didn't give a damn anymore.

I wouldn't walk away, not after everything I'd been through. Not after all our sacrifices. Whatever happened next, it would determine the fate of every person in this colony, maybe even beyond.

We had a right to *live*. To hell with anyone who tried to tell me otherwise.

If these Celestials meant to take what we'd earned, I'd fight them for as long as I was able. If it meant proving Brigham right, so be it.

That was my nature. It was in my very blood.

I was made to be free, and I'd be damned if I was going to let anyone tell me otherwise. Brigham, the Union, Celestials, gods, or men.

None of them would take ownership over my soul.

"Alright, then, boys," I said, pushing my chair back and getting to my feet. "I think it's time we got to work."

Jace, Abigail, and Lex return in RENEGADE CHILDREN, available now on Amazon.

Read on for a special note from the author.

AUTHOR NOTES

The Eternals Arc is in full swing! I hope you enjoyed the beginning of the next chapter in the Renegade storyline. I really wanted to show a different side of Jace for this book. He's gone through so much that we expect him to roll with the punches, but even the bravest of us has a fear inside of them, trying to eat them from within. It's only when we rise to the challenge and face that ghost that we grow stronger. In Jace's case, he had to move on from his fight with Brigham and let go of his paranoia, even though that same paranoia had kept him alive for so long.

Turns out, of course, that he was sort of right, although for the wrong reasons. It wasn't the Union he had to fear, but something far more dangerous. A brand new threat with unparalleled power. The Celestials.

The next book will see our fearless crew confront this mysterious group, expanding the mythos of the Renegade universe more than ever before. It's something I've wanted to delve into for a while now, so I'm stoked to finally be able to explore it.

That being said, I'm also working on other stories in

this universe that fall outside of the main storyline and Jace's perspective. For starters, I'm working on an Abigail origin book. You may have noticed some references to her backstory in this book, including her sister. All of that is going to be revealed in the origin novel, coming later this year. Don't worry, though, the main Renegade series will continue to release at a steady pace. It is still my top priority.

Oh, and before I forget, we had a few new faces pop up in this entry, including Petra and Verne. They will both return in the next installment, along with Freddie (in case you were worried that he was getting sidelined). Petra will be especially fun, thanks her brand new mechanized arm. 😉

Until next time, Renegades,

J.N. Chaney

PS. Amazon won't tell you when the next Renegade book will come out, but there are several ways you can stay informed.

1) **Fly on over to the Facebook group, JN Chaney's Renegade Readers**, and say hello. It's a great place to hang with other sarcastic sci-fi readers who don't mind a good laugh.

2) **Follow me directly on Amazon**. To do this, head to the **store page** for this book (or my Amazon author profile) and click the Follow button beneath my picture.

That will prompt Amazon to notify you when I release a new book. You'll just need to check your emails.

3) **You can join my mailing list by clicking here**. This will allow me to stay in touch with you directly, and you'll also receive a free copy of The Other Side of Nowhere.

Doing one of these or **all three** (for best results) will ensure you know every time a new entry in *The Renegade Star* series is published. Please take a moment to do one of these so you'll be able to join Jace, Abigail, and Lex on their next galaxy-spanning adventure.

THE RENEGADE STAR UNIVERSE

Available on Amazon

The Renegade Star Series

They say the Earth is just a myth. Something to tell your children when you put them to sleep, the lost homeworld of humanity. Everyone knows it isn't real, though. It can't be.

But when Captain Jace Hughes encounters a nun with a mysterious piece of cargo and a bold secret, he soon discovers that everything he thought he knew about Earth is wrong. So very, very wrong.

Climb aboard The Renegade Star and assemble a crew, follow the clues, uncover the truth, and most importantly, try to stay alive.

The Last Reaper Series

When a high value scientist is taken hostage inside the galaxy's most dangerous prison, Halek Cain is the only man for the job.

The last remaining survivor of the Reaper program, Hal is an unstoppable force of fuel and madness. A veteran amputee-turned-cyborg, he has a history of violence and a talent for killing that is unmatched by any soldier.

With the promise of freedom as his only incentive, he'll stop at nothing to earn back his life from the people who made him, imprisoned him, and were too afraid to let him die.

The Orion Colony Series

Humanity's Exodus is about to begin.

When half of mankind revolts and demands more opportunity, those at the top decide on a compromise: they will build the first colony ships and allow those who are willing to discover new worlds to leave and start over.

Twelve ships are built, the first of which is called Orion. Many are eager to go, but only one hundred thousand are chosen for each vessel. Far from Earth, a new life awaits, and it promises the prosperity they've always wanted.

But still, resistance stirs, eager to sabotage this new expansion effort, threatening the promise of a new life. As Orion moves through the void of space, towards a distant world, its passengers must fight for survival in an unprecedented conflict.

Win or lose, their future will be forever changed.

The Fifth Column Series

After a soldier is left for dead, Eva Delgado's life begins to unravel.

The truth of what happened remains a mystery, and the government will stop at nothing to keep it buried.

Together with the unit's medic, Eva finds herself branded a terrorist and enemy of the State, hunted by two opposing governments.

When the pair uncover a plot that could have ramifications for the whole galaxy, they know they have to act, but it will take all of their training, cunning and just a bit of luck to do what no one else has achieved.

But what do you do when every secret begets another? And how far will you go to find the truth?

Nameless (Abigail's Story)

Abigail and Clementine were just a couple of orphans looking for a home.

But when the two girls witness something terrible, they have no choice but to leave their orphanage and go into hiding. The only person willing to take them in is a man named Mulberry, but his home isn't the safest place for two innocent children.

Abigail and Clementine quickly discover that their new caretaker is the head of a guild of assassins, and the two are thrown into a whole new world of danger. To survive, they'll need to adapt, focus, and learn how to survive in a world of killers.

The Constable (Alphonse's Story)

My name is Alphonse Malloy, and I see everything.

From a simple glance, I know your hobbies, what you ate for breakfast, how well you slept, and whether or not your wife is secretly seeing the high school biology teacher when you're not around.

I can't explain how or why I get these feelings, only that I know they're true.

All the little secrets you're too afraid to tell.

Sometimes, that means helping people. Other times, it means staring down the barrel of a loaded gun.

I wish I could tell you I was using this ability for good.

I wish I could tell you a lot of things.

The Constable Returns

Alphonse Malloy may just be the smartest man alive.

A year has passed since Alphonse joined the Constables, but his work is only just beginning. In order to graduate and achieve full Constable status, Alphonse will need to complete one final mission.

When new information about an old enemy arises, Al and his mentor Dorian must head deep into the Deadlands in search of answers.

But in a galaxy of secrets, the truth is often more elusive than it seems.

As the search continues, Alphonse's talents will be pushed to their absolute limit, and he'll need everything he's learned to make it out of this one alive.

Warrior Queen (Lucia's Story)

On a lost world, far removed from Earth, a group of humans struggle to survive.

Two thousand years after their ancestors lost control of a hidden genetics research facility, the descendants of mankind have been reduced to a tribe of two hundred survivors. They fight, kill, and die in an endless cycle, all in the hope that things will get better.

Lucia is one of these colonists and the daughter of the tribe's leader, the Director. Together with several other candidates, she must soon undergo a trial to decide her father's replacement. The winner will shape the future of the entire colony.

But the trial is dangerous, meant to test each candidate's wits and strengths to see who is truly worthy. To claim victory, Lucia will need to venture out into the tunnels near the city to search for lost artifacts known as Cores--small but powerful devices capable of harnessing endless energy.

But there are monsters here, waiting in the dark, and they are always hungry. Beware the Boneclaw, Lucia's father use to tell her, for it lives only to kill and to feed.

Lucia must do whatever it takes, learn as much as she can, and fight with every ounce of strength if she hopes to make it through the day.

Forget winning the trial. The real challenge is staying alive.

Resonant Son Series

30 floors of nightmare fueled action. An ex-cop with nothing left to lose.

After losing his job and family, Flint Reed finds himself in the middle of a terrorist attack. With nothing but his wits and experience as a former Union police officer, he must do everything he can to stay alive.

As he soon discovers, however, there are also hostages, and no one is coming to save them.

All hope falls to Flint.

But as he fights to navigate the building, the real answers begin to unravel. What are the terrorists really after, and why are they so intent on getting into the vault?

Experience the beginning of the Resonant Son series. If you're a fan of Die Hard, Renegade Star, or the Last Reaper, you'll love this epic scifi thrill ride.

Galactic Law Series

Lethal force is authorized.

In the wild space of the Deadlands, Taurus Station is where miners and tourists come to play, and the ravager gangs follow close behind. Out here, far from the civilized world, the Law has a name.

Gage Walker is the son of hard-nosed asteroid miners. Brash, rough, and crude, he's one of the few deputies working the station.

Still a rookie, Walker is tasked with the security of a mining magnate's daughter, an easy job that quickly takes a turn for the worst.

The ravager gangs want her, and it falls to Walker to find out why.

In a chase across Taurus Station, Deputy Walker must prove he's fit to wear the badge and issue his own form of justice...*one body at a time.*

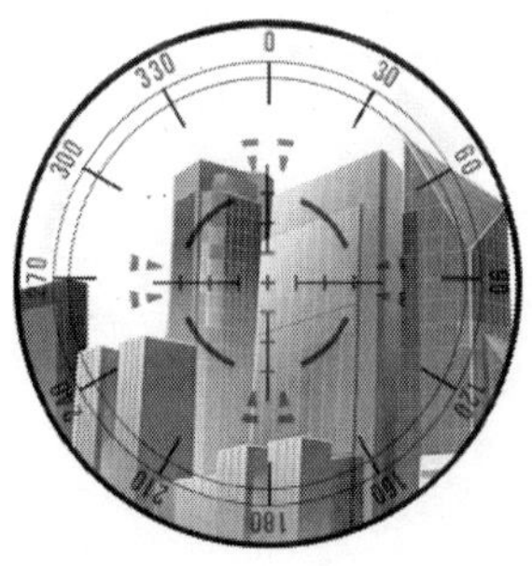

Deadland Drifter Series

When a dental appointment goes sideways, former Union Operative Jack Burner wakes to find himself drugged, and imprisoned.

And he's given a choice: assassinate an Admiral... or allow himself to be killed.

With no other option, Jack reluctantly accepts the mission, only to find himself being trailed by a mysterious blonde woman... and she may or may not want him dead.

As if dealing with a terrorist group wasn't enough.

With the fate of the Admiral and thousands of lives on hanging in the balance, Jack stands in the middle of an event that could ignite a war on the edge of the Deadlands and Union Space.

Despite his exceptional abilities, training, and tenancy, even Jack has little to no chance of preventing this particular powder keg from exploding.

He's going to need a miracle.

The Renegade Series

Jace Hughes is a Renegade.

That means taking jobs and not asking questions, whether that involves smuggling, transporting runnaways, or performing other, far less wholesome work. Whatever the situation, Jace is willing to do what it takes to achieve his dream and live the life he's always wanted.

That is, until he comes face to face with an item of unprecedented value—something that could give him everything he needs to pay off his debt and be free.

The only problem is that selling it would also shift the balance of power between the two largest empires in the galaxy.

And spark another intergalactic war.

Unfortunately for Jace, he won't have long to decide. Renegades, assassins, and government cronies are after the item, too, and unlike Jace, they won't hesitate to kill.

CONNECT WITH J.N. CHANEY

Don't miss out on these exclusive perks:

- Instant access to free short stories from series like *The Messenger*, *Starcaster,* and more.
- Receive email updates for new releases and other news.
- Get notified when we run special deals on books and audiobooks.

So, what are you waiting for? Enter your email address at the link below to stay in the loop.

https://www.jnchaney.com/renegade-subscribe

JOIN THE CONVERSATION

Join the conversation and get updates on new and upcoming releases in the awesomely active **Facebook group**, "JN Chaney's Renegade Readers."

This is a hotspot where readers come together and share their lives and interests, discuss the series, and speak directly to J.N. Chaney and his co-authors.

facebook.com/groups/jnchaneyreaders

PREVIEW: THE AMBER PROJECT

Documents of Historical, Scientific, and Cultural Significance
Play Audio Transmission File 021
Recorded April 19, 2157

CARTWRIGHT: *This is Lieutenant Colonel Felix Cartwright. It's been a week since my last transmission and two months since the day we found the city…the day the world fell apart. If anyone can hear this, please respond.*

If you're out there, no doubt you know about the gas. You might think you're all that's left. But if you're receiving this, let me assure you, you are not alone. There are people here. Hundreds, in fact, and for now, we're safe. If you can make it here, you will be, too.

The city's a few miles underground, not far from El Rico Air Force Base. That's where my people came from. As always, the coordi-

nates are attached. If anyone gets this, please respond. Let us know you're there…that you're still alive.

End Audio File

April 14, 2339
Maternity District

MILES BELOW THE SURFACE OF THE EARTH, deep within the walls of the last human city, a little boy named Terry played quietly with his sister in a small two-bedroom apartment.

Today was his very first birthday. He was turning seven.

"What's a birthday?" his sister Janice asked, tugging at his shirt. She was only four years old and had recently taken to following her big brother everywhere he went. "What does it mean?"

Terry smiled, eager to explain. "Mom says when you turn seven, you get a birthday. It means you grow up and get to start school. It's a pretty big deal."

"When will I get a birthday?"

"You're only four, so you have to wait."

"I wish I was seven," she said softly, her thin black hair hanging over her eyes. "I want to go with you."

He got to his feet and began putting the toy blocks away. They had built a castle together on the floor, but

Mother would yell if they left a mess. "I'll tell you all about it when I get home. I promise, okay?"

"Okay!" she said cheerily and proceeded to help.

Right at that moment, the speaker next to the door let out a soft chime, followed by their mother's voice. "Downstairs, children," she said. "Hurry up now."

Terry took his sister's hand. "Come on, Jan," he said.

She frowned, squeezing his fingers. "Okay."

They arrived downstairs, their mother nowhere to be found.

"She's in the kitchen," Janice said, pointing at the farthest wall. "See the light-box?"

Terry looked at the locator board, although his sister's name for it worked just as well. It was a map of the entire apartment, with small lights going on and off in different colors, depending on which person was in which room. *There's us*, he thought, *green for me and blue for Janice, and there's Mother in red*. Terry never understood why they needed something like that because of how small the apartment was, but every family got one, or so Mother had said.

As he entered the kitchen, his mother stood at the far counter sorting through some data on her pad. "What's that?" he asked.

"Something for work," she said. She tapped the front of the pad and placed it in her bag. "Come on, Terrance, we've got to get you ready and out the door. Today's your first day, after all, and we have to make a good impression."

"When will he be back?" asked Janice.

"Hurry up. Let's go, Terrance," she said, ignoring the question. She grabbed his hand and pulled him along. "We have about twenty minutes to get all the way to the education district. Hardly enough time at all." Her voice was sour. He had noticed it more and more lately, as the weeks went on, ever since a few months ago when that man from the school came to visit. His name was Mr. Huxley, one of the few men who Terry ever had the chance to talk to, and from the way Mother acted—she was so agitated—he must have been important.

"Terrance." His mother's voice pulled him back. "Stop moping and let's go."

Janice ran and hugged him, wrapping her little arms as far around him as she could. "Love you," she said.

"Love you too."

"Bye," she said shyly.

He kissed her forehead and walked to the door, where his mother stood talking with the babysitter, Ms. Cartwright. "I'll only be a few hours," Mother said. "If it takes any longer, I'll message you."

"Don't worry about a thing, Mara," Ms. Cartwright assured her. "You take all the time you need."

Mother turned to him. "There you are," she said, taking his hand. "Come on, or we'll be late."

As they left the apartment, Mother's hand tugging him along, Terry tried to imagine what might happen at school today. Would it be like his home lessons? Would he be behind the other children, or was everything new? He enjoyed learning, but there was still a chance the school might be too hard for him. What would he do? Mother had taught him some things, like algebra and English, but who knew how far along the other kids were by now?

Terry walked quietly down the overcrowded corridors with an empty, troubled head. He hated this part of the district. So many people on the move, brushing against him, like clothes in an overstuffed closet.

He raised his head, nearly running into a woman and her baby. She had wrapped the child in a green and brown cloth, securing it against her chest. "Excuse me," he said, but the lady ignored him.

His mother paused and looked around. "Terrance, what are you doing? I'm over here," she said, spotting him.

"Sorry."

They waited together for the train, which was running a few minutes behind today.

"I wish they'd hurry up," said a nearby lady. She was young, about fifteen years old. "Do you think it's because of the outbreak?"

"Of course," said a much older woman. "Some of the trains are busy carrying contractors to the slums to patch the walls. It slows the others down because now they have to make more stops."

"I heard fourteen workers died. Is it true?"

"You know how the gas is," she said. "It's very quick. Thank God for the quarantine barriers."

Suddenly, there was a loud smashing sound, followed by

three long beeps. It echoed through the platform for a moment, vibrating along the walls until it was gone. Terry flinched, squeezing his mother's hand.

"Ouch," she said. "Terrance, relax."

"But the sound," he said.

"It's the contractors over there." She pointed to the other side of the tracks, far away from them. It took a moment for Terry to spot them, but once he did, it felt obvious. Four of them stood together. Their clothes were orange, with no clear distinction between their shirts and their pants, and on each of their heads was a solid red plastic hat. Three of them were holding tools, huddled against a distant wall. They were reaching inside of it, exchanging tools every once in a while, until eventually the fourth one called them to back away. As they made some room, steam rose from the hole, with a puddle of dark liquid forming at the base. The fourth contractor handled a machine several feet from the others, which had three legs and rose to his chest. He waved the other four to stand near him and pressed the pad on the machine. Together, the contractors watched as the device flashed a series of small bright lights. It only lasted a few seconds. Once it was over, they gathered close to the wall again and resumed their work.

"What are they doing?" Terry asked.

His mother looked down at him. "What? Oh, they're fixing the wall, that's all."

"Why?" he asked.

"Probably because there was a shift last night. Remember when the ground shook?"

Yeah, I remember, he thought. *It woke me up*. "So they're fixing it?"

"Yes, right." She sighed and looked around. "Where is that damned train?"

Terry tugged on her hand. "That lady over there said it's late because of the gas."

His mother looked at him. "What did you say?"

"The lady…the one right there." He pointed to the younger girl a few feet away. "She said the gas came, so that's why the trains are slow. It's because of the slums." He paused a minute. "No, wait. It's because they're *going* to the slums."

His mother stared at the girl, turning back to the tracks and saying nothing.

"Mother?" he said.

"Be quiet for a moment, Terrance."

Terry wanted to ask her what was wrong, or if he had done anything to upset her, but he knew when to stay silent. So he left it alone like she wanted. Just like a good little boy.

The sound of the arriving train filled the platform with such horrific noise that it made Terry's ears hurt. The train, still vibrating as he stepped onboard, felt like it was alive.

After a short moment, the doors closed. The train was moving.

Terry didn't know if the shaking was normal or not. Mother had taken him up to the medical wards on this train once when he was younger, but never again after that. He didn't remember much about it, except that he liked it. The medical wards were pretty close to where he lived, a few stops before the labs, and several stops before the education district. After that, the train ran through Pepper Plaza, then the food farms and Housing Districts 04 through 07 and finally the outer ring factories and the farms. As Terry stared at the route map on the side of the train wall, memorizing what he could of it, he tried to imagine all the places he could go and the things he might see. What kind of shops did the shopping plaza have, for example, and what was it like to work on the farms? Maybe one day he could go and find out for himself—ride the train all day to see everything there was to see. Boy, wouldn't that be something?

"Departure call: 22-10, education district," erupted the com in its monotone voice. It took only a moment before the train began to slow.

"That's us. Come on," said Mother. She grasped his hand, pulling him through the doors before they were fully opened.

Almost to the school, Terry thought. He felt warm suddenly. Was he getting nervous? And why now? He'd known about this forever, and it was only hitting him *now*?

He kept taking shorter breaths. He wanted to pull away and return home, but Mother's grasp was tight and firm, and the closer they got to the only major building in the area, the tighter and firmer it became.

Now that he was there, now that the time had finally come, a dozen questions ran through Terry's mind. Would the other kids like him? What if he wasn't as smart as everyone else? Would they make fun of him? He had no idea what to expect.

Terry swallowed, the lump in his throat nearly choking him.

An older man stood at the gate of the school's entrance. He dressed in an outfit that didn't resemble any of the clothes in Terry's district or even on the trains. A gray uniform—the color of the pavement, the walls, and the streets—matched his silver hair to the point where it was difficult to tell where one ended and the other began. "Ah," he said. "Mara, I see you've brought another student. I was wondering when we'd meet the next one. Glad to see you're still producing. It's been, what? Five or six years? Something like that, I think."

"Yes, thank you, this is Terrance," said Mother quickly. "I was told there would be an escort." She paused, glancing over the man and through the windows. "Where's Bishop? He assured me he'd be here for this."

"The *colonel,*" he corrected, "is in his office, and the boy is to be taken directly to him as soon as I have registered his arrival."

She let out a frustrated sigh. "He was supposed to meet me at the gate for this himself. I wanted to talk to him about a few things."

"What's wrong?" Terry asked.

She looked down at him. "Oh, it's nothing, don't worry. You have to go inside now, that's all."

"You're not coming in?"

"I'm afraid not," said the man. "She's not permitted."

"It's all right," Mother said, cupping her hand over his cheek. "They'll take care of you in there."

But it's just school, Terry thought. "I'll see you tonight, though, right?"

She bent down and embraced him tightly, more than she had in a long time. He couldn't help but relax. "I'm sorry, Terrance. Please be careful up there. I know you don't understand it now, but you will eventually. Everything will be fine." She rose, releasing his hand for the first time since they left the train. "So that's it?" Mother said to the man.

"Yes, ma'am."

"Good." She turned and walked away, pausing a moment as she reached the corner and continued until she was out of sight.

The man pulled out a board with a piece of paper on it. "When you go through here, head straight to the back of the hall. A guard there will take you to see Colonel Bishop. Just do what they say and answer everything with either 'Yes, sir' or 'No, sir,' and you'll be fine. Understand?"

Terry didn't understand, but he nodded anyway.

The man pushed open the door with his arm and leg, holding it there and waiting. "Right through here you go," he said.

Terry entered, reluctantly, and the door closed quickly behind him.

The building, full of the same metal and shades of brown and gray that held together the rest of the city, rose higher than any other building Terry had ever been in. Around the room, perched walkways circled the walls, cluttered with doors and hallways that branched off into unknown regions. Along the walkways, dozens of people walked back and forth as busily as they had in the train station. More importantly, Terry quickly realized, most of them were men.

For so long, the only men he had seen were the maintenance workers who came and went or the occasional teacher who visited the children when they were nearing their birthdays. It was so rare to see any men at all, especially in such great numbers. *Maybe they're all teachers*, he thought. They weren't dressed like the workers: white coats and some with brown jackets—thick jackets with laced boots and bodies as stiff as the walls. Maybe that was what teachers wore. How could he know? He had never met one besides Mr. Huxley, and that was months ago.

"Well, don't just stand there gawking," said a voice from the other end of the room. It was another man, dressed the same as the others. "Go on in through here." He pointed to another door, smaller than the one Terry had entered from. "Everyone today gets to meet the colonel. Go on now. Hurry up. You don't want to keep him waiting."

Terry did as the man said and stepped through the

doorway, his footsteps clanking against the hard metal floor, echoing through what sounded like the entire building.

"Well, come in, why don't you?" came a voice from inside.

Terry stepped cautiously into the room, which was much nicer than the entranceway. It was clean, at least compared to some of the other places Terry had been, including his own home. The walls held several shelves, none of which lacked for any company of things. Various ornaments caught Terry's eye, like the little see-through globe on the shelf nearest to the door, which held a picture of a woman's face inside, although some of it was faded and hard to make out. There was also a crack in it. What purpose could such a thing have? Terry couldn't begin to guess. Next to it lay a frame with a small, round piece of metal inside of it. An inscription below the glass read, "U.S. Silver Dollar, circa 2064." Terry could easily read the words, but he didn't understand them. What was this thing? And why was it so important that it needed to be placed on a shelf for everyone to look at?

"I said come in," said Bishop abruptly. He sat at the far end of the room behind a large brown desk. Terry had forgotten he was even there. "I didn't mean for you to stop at the door. Come over here."

Terry hurried closer, stopping a few feet in front of the desk.

"I'm Colonel Bishop. You must be Terrance," said the man. "I've been wondering when you were going to show up." He wore a pair of thin glasses and had one of the larger pads in his hand. "Already seven. Imagine that."

"Yes, sir," Terry said, remembering the doorman's words.

The colonel was a stout man, a little wider than the others. He was older too, Terry guessed. He may have been tall, but it was difficult to tell without seeing his whole body. "I expect you're hoping to begin your classes now," said Bishop.

"Yes, sir," he said.

"You say that, but you don't really know what you're saying yes to, do you?"

The question seemed more like a statement, so Terry didn't answer. He only stood there. Who was this man? Was this how school was supposed to be?

"Terrance, let me ask you something," said the colonel, taking a moment. "Did your mother tell you anything about this program you're going into?"

Terry thought about the question for a moment. "Um, she said you come to school on your birthday," he said. "And that it's just like it is at home, except there's more kids like me."

Colonel Bishop blinked. "That's right, I suppose. What else did she say?"

"That when it was over, I get to go back home," he said.

"And when did she say that was?"

Terry didn't answer.

Colonel Bishop cocked an eyebrow. "Well? Didn't she say?"

"No, sir," muttered Terry.

The man behind the desk started chuckling. "So you don't know how long you're here for?"

"No, sir."

Colonel Bishop set the pad in his hand down. "Son, you're here for the next ten years."

A sudden rush swelled up in Terry's chest and face. What was Bishop talking about? Of course Terry was going home. He couldn't stay here. "But I promised my sister I'd be home today," he said. "I have to go back."

"Too bad," said the colonel. "Your mother really did you a disservice by not telling you. But don't worry. We just have to get you started." He tapped the pad on his desk, and the door opened. A cluster of footsteps filled the hall before two large men appeared, each wearing the same brown coats as the rest. "Well, that was fast," he said.

One of the men saluted. "Yes, sir. No crying with the last one. Took her right to her room without incident."

Terry wanted to ask who *the last one* was, and why it should be a good thing that she didn't cry. Did other kids cry when they came to this school? What kind of place *was* this?

"Well, hopefully, Terrence here will do the same," said Bishop. He looked at Terry. "Right? You're not going to give us any trouble, are you?"

Terry didn't know what to do or what to say. All he

could think about was getting far away from here. He didn't want to go with the men. He didn't want to behave. All he wanted to do was go home.

But he couldn't, not anymore. He was here in this place with nowhere to go. No way out. He wanted to scream, to yell at the man behind the desk and his two friends, and tell them about how stupid it was for them to do what they were doing.

He opened his mouth to explain, to scream as loud as he could that he wouldn't go. But in that moment, the memory of the doorman came back to him, and instead of yelling, he repeated the words he'd been told before. "No, sir," he said softly.

Bishop smiled, nodding at the two men in the doorway. "Exactly what I like to hear."

SERIES BY J.N. CHANEY

The Variant Saga

Renegade Star Series

Renegade Standalones

Orion Colony Series *(with Jonathan Yanez)*

The Last Reaper Series *(with Scott Moon)*

The Fifth Column Series *(with Molly Lerma)*

Resonant Son Series *(with Christopher Hopper)*

Galactic Law Series *(with James S. Aaron)*

Deadland Drifter Series *(with Ell Leigh Clarke)*

Ruins of the Galaxy Series *(with Christopher Hopper)*

Ruins of the Earth Series *(with Christopher Hopper)*

The Messenger Series *(with Terry Maggert)*

Starcaster Series *(with Terry Maggert)*

Sol Arbiter Series *(with Jia Shen)*

Exodus Ark Series

Cyborg Corp Series *(with Chris Winder)*

Wayward Galaxy Series *(with Jason Anspach)*

King's League Series *(with Jason Anspach)*

Orphan Wars Series *(with Scott Moon)*

Sentenced to War Series *(with Jonathan P. Brazee)*

Standalones:

Their Solitary Way

The Other Side of Nowhere

Forever Family

ABOUT THE AUTHOR

J. N. Chaney has a Master of Fine Arts in creative writing and fancies himself quite the Super Mario Bros. fan. When he isn't writing or gaming, you can find him online at **www.jnchaney.com**.

He migrates often but was last seen in Avon Park, Florida. Any sightings should be reported, as they are rare.

Renegade Dawn is his twelfth novel.

Manufactured by Amazon.ca
Acheson, AB

12564276R00176